the tale of
enigmas

stories beyond the originality

The Tale of Enigmas
Edited & Compiled by Srishti Sareen
Print Edition

First Published in India in 2021
Inkfeathers Publishing
New Delhi 110095

ISBN 978-81-950205-6-0

www.inkfeathers.com

the tale of
enigmas

stories beyond the originality

Edited & Compiled by

Srishti Sareen

Inkfeathers Publishing

DISCLAIMER

The anthology "The Tale of Enigmas" is a collection of 30 stories by 24 authors who belong to different parts of the globe. The anthology editor and the publisher have edited the content provided by the co-authors to enhance the experience for readers and make it free of plagiarism as much as possible. Unless otherwise indicated, all the names, characters, objects, businesses, places, events, incidents- whether physical/non-physical, real/unreal, tangible/ intangible in whatsoever description used in this book are either the product of the author's imagination or used in a fictitious manner. Any resemblance to actual persons, objects, entities, living or dead, or actual events is purely coincidental. The stories published in this book are solely owned by their respective authors and are no way intended to hurt anyone's religious, political, spiritual, brand, personal or fanatic beliefs and/or faith, whatsoever.

In case, any sort of plagiarism is detected in the stories within this anthology or in case of any complaints or grievances or objections, neither the anthology editor, nor the publisher are to be held responsible for any such claims. The author(s) who holds the rights to the story/stories, shall be held responsible, whatsoever.

CO-AUTHORED BY

Tejasvee Nagar | Deepika Ganu | Karen Pereira | Rosalind Reshma | Anamika Kundu | Prajitha Ravipati | Vaibhav Koktare | Kanchan Hiranandani | Rutika Pandya | Swikriti Lahoty | Dipali Talwar | Muskan Kamwani | Shaymi Shah | Manoj Vaz | Honey Patel | Nitya Saini | Mansi Gupta | Dewni De Silva | Ranjna Gopal | Munmun Aidasani | Sumeet Doondani | Vaishali Chandorkar Chitale | Vishakha Naware | Kristin Carmen

CONTENTS

Srishti Sareen

Srishti Sareen is a student of Bachelor of Commerce. She is born and brought up in Ludhiana. Writing is what makes her feel alive and relieved. She started writing when she was in 10th standard, and never got over the era of satisfaction ever again. She thinks that penning things down and expressing yourself is a better and simpler way to exhibit the rough things happening around you, because in the end, people will come up with awful phrases just to make you feel lesser of themselves. Moreover, she always says, "No matter how it started or when it started a day spent with your pen and journal is worth spending time with and it will always be."

EDITOR'S NOTE

Having a name on this book is still unbelievable. The way I let my guard down out of nowhere and did these unplanned things is surreal. When my shell cracked up for the options to pursue things that were beyond the plan. Reading all these stories and compiling them will always be close to my heart.

Creating my own little family here has been a hell of a ride. It is all because these beautiful people, these writers, made it happen. All of you gave me the strength to never let it go. That's why we are holding this book in our hands right now. It would be impossible to achieve what we just did.

All these 30 thrilling stories made me feel every single word differently. All these stories had originality and are worth reading. Every story had something hidden deep underneath that made me crave more to know what happened next. I hope you all will love reading all these stories to find out what this little bag of pixie dust beholds for you to unravel.

Love,

Srishti Sareen

1

At 12:00 AM, We See The Difference

by Tejasvee Nagar

Midnight: a bridge between what is to come and what has passed. In this moment, they say, you leave the old chapters, the stale pages behind and start afresh. Waiting for the morning sun to burn, you surrender yourself to the night.

A small meek hand reached towards the bookshelf, a sloth smile whispered – this is for you 'Melancholy Jacques'. Tresa Neveris, a keen literature enthusiast picked up the oldest book from the rack: Dramas by Shakespeare. There were no bookmarks kept between the pages, but she could easily tell which yellowish ochre page was Scene Two: Act Seven of 'As You Like It.' Sipping hot coffee, she spoke to herself, "All the world's a stage, and all the men and women merely players."

That night Tresa had just stepped out of the oblivion. Into the darkness, she was hustling with the bushes unknown of who she was turning into. The shadows of the night could never let her sleep, neither did Anna Glace.

She returned at 2:00 that night, drowned in melancholy. She disapproved of everything. She wanted to close the chapter of Anna Glace forever but she couldn't. *What if Anna had an actual future?* she thought. A future that would change everything and make things hopeful. "Tresa you are a false believer. You believe I live within you. I don't. How much would you tremble with time, honey?" Anna had once said. Tresa was tired at how much Anna, a creation of her own, a character from her novel – 'We are all Jokers' was overpowering her. It has gotten so bad that at times while talking to somebody she could not make out whether the one responding was her or Anna.

Meanwhile, Tresa's monologues were meaningless, they said. She would become breathless every time she would try to speak. She would be cold. It was her story that they were a part of but its characters gave her a motive. The characters were breathing life into Tresa. The characters were making her a puppet, controlling her strings. The morning sun approached the dawn. Tresa should be proud of herself that she survived the previous night. She walked to school with her backpack, loaded with twenty different books. She would complete her homework at school. She had to. The question was, would Anna let her do that anytime soon?

She studied at the library with Genesis James, a good friend of hers. He was someone who could conclude by the look of an eye what was soaring into the skies of Tresa. The skies were her blue eyes, the one for which poems should have been penned. Who would do that task when the poet by heart was actually Tresa?

Just then Genesis found a red book with no papers inside it.

"Tresa!" He exclaimed. He couldn't contain the excitement to hear answers to what was going inside her mind.

"What? Gem, we need to study right now. There is no stopwatch to stop the time. People around me are aware of my chameleon nature. You don't want them to see that, right? Things are so confusing."

Tresa spoke in the softest voice as if the secret was treasured by Gem and her, not even the walls. He noticed that something had vanished,

"Your letters to yourself? Where are those pages?" He intervened directly.

Gone with the wind,

Clustered into the sky.

Ashes that are not dust,

The sheath that covers me is a lie.

Tresa covered depth in a mere sentence, she hinted at many things.

"Tresa! Your computer journal shows an error. It isn't a coincidence, right? What about the actual drafts about your letters to yourself?" Gem spoke so fast, that no one could have sustained his audacity.

"Gem, I do not want you to look in the dark the way I do. I don't know, it always interests me, more than scaring me. I am petrified of not being able to figure out things. Is there a reason for who I am?"

She needed to be hugged, she needed to break down and whisper her sobs.

"Tresa honey, can we rekindle about the greatest authors, having the darkest characters. What would Anna be without you? Stop believing in Anna. Just be who you are. It would be tough to let go of the first character that you ever created, but what am I here for? We would work on a new story. Right from 12 AM. Right from the beginning. Okay?"

Gem knew how his words warmed Tresa's heart. His hug was even more intense, he never wanted to let her go. He was always there for her.

The next day, they were back to grind. It felt impossible to let Anna back off easily. They had methods and measures. By evening, Tresa and Gem spoke out dialogues. One day, she was Margo Roth Spiegelman from Paper Towns. The next day she was Hermione Granger. Everything went swiftly, and Anna went away. This time for real, forever.

Tresa was waiting at the school library for Gem. She wanted to hug him tightly and wanted him to know, he is her whole world. She got a letter, from a classmate of his. Tresa looked at the letter and read it while her heart cried. She wasn't able to express what just happened.

The letter read,

"Something has changed, not in you but in me. I wanted to let you know that I can't write long words like you, but you were becoming the north pole star. I wanted to discover the stars and the sky, a necessary leave from everything and you. Please don't approach me, distraction."

Tresa never believed it was him, but she was quick at reading manuscripts. The question was, what happened in a day? What made him do that? What made him drift away? He was the only one who was closest to me yesterday and today, he asks me to not even approach him anymore? There were thousands of questions running in her head like a mixtape. Gem knew what he did. Gem knew how it would affect her fragile heart. Gem should have discussed everything about this with her but he didn't.

What was the reason?

Tresa couldn't hold his confused mind. All her thumbnail sketches were left scribbled in her diary.

She jumped back to writing poems,

Never trust someone completely,

Never let them know your weakness.

Whether it is a phase complementary,

No one deserves to be "Yours Dearly."

Gem had not only left a stain on her heart but a stain on those characters too. By half-round around the sun, everyone around her had already considered her as a maniac. They could notice how she would be a chameleon at times.

She wrote, "I shouted for Gem, but he didn't come. He was close to me, but he pretended he was that farthest star I had ever aimed for."

Her diary was back again to the town when those existing bees spread the rumours of how Tresa fell for Gem's kind heart, and he left her due to the nuisance. "The Assumera" bullies of the town weren't good to her. She had to bring down another character, it was the right time. The right song on the radio. The right melancholy. Allen Mystic was created. Tresa breathed life to her, Tresa lived her character. Tresa looked at those haunted ballrooms, and she went in for her monologues.

She had to bring Den Cluster. The antagonist to Allen Mystic. Den Cluster was an enemy, she believed. He took over her ability to write. Den Cluster could have toiled near Allen's house until he got those exact words that were needed to put Allen into a dilemma. The thumbnail sketch resembled Genesis James, the verbal sketch was more similar. Tresa's room belonged to Allen Mystic.

"Den what is your problem? Why don't you let me be myself?"

"You surely need to stop being what you are! Your words have no symphony! You don't even know where you are leading." Den screamed.

Allen sobbed, and her heart was heavy.

She lost everything in a year but she released her new novel, named 'Losing A Gem, Winning Over Myself.'

A year passed, and her heart that hustled was calm. It was a phase. A phase to bring in Den Cluster to reality. Genesis James was real and Den Cluster was what filled her mind with every possible misconception.

Genesis James still didn't disapprove of his word. When he said, he would never meet Tresa Neveris again, he meant it.

A year passed and Tresa would've been at calm the entire day like usual but just then, when the horizon was touching the mountain bidding a timely farewell to the sun, Tresa met Genesis James. In the same park, at the same time.

The silent park where no one visited. A part and parcel of Gem and Tresa's life.

Gem watched Tresa drowning in the same blue pond and saved her.

"Tresa? What are you doing? Are you out of your mind?"

"Go away, Den!" She sputtered the water stopping her to inhale.

"Tresa. It's me Gem. Your friend, remember?" Gem assured.

"Don't call yourself that Den. You have been my worst enemy. You are coming to life, just like any other character.

Just like someone I would never hold. Just like my heart that is filled with so many grudges."

Tresa was Allen, she repeatedly asked Gem to go away, as if he was Den.

"Okay, Allen. Do you know what makes me your enemy? The thought that I went off in the middle, being selfish for I couldn't handle the power you held. I couldn't recognize whether I wanted to stop you from being you because you would have made a better conclusion.

Allen was surprised by the instant dialogue delivery and never thought the dark shadow she talked to was bright in real.

Tresa would not have returned, but now it was Gem to snatch her out. Nothing was submerged, everything was floating on their boat.

"You can't hurt me, can you?" She whispered.

"I would never hurt you. I hurt my mind. I hurt my heart, I'm already wounded for not coming back. I never wanted to be the extraversion of your wound. I wanted you to live free. I have been known to beat 'The Assumera' up for spreading the wrong word." It was Gem back to real, and Den was just a piece in Tresa's mind.

"Gem, this time. I have not known myself crazy for reasoning." Tresa mumbled.

Gem looked into her eyes and kissed her, touching her soul.

It was the right time to accept and take in the right treatment for the characters. They would stay with the writer, and not turn to realistic fairies or monsters.

Tresa recited her poem - the last one she wrote in the ballroom thinking about Den to be Gem. This time Allen,

Anna, and Den were characters controlled by Tresa and Gem, not vice versa.

You can't predict personalities,
You can't read minds.
Behind every surreal lie,
There's a sheath of unacceptable truth to find.

2

Life Is An Enigma

by Deepika Ganu

"What are you talking about?" Diya asked with fear and uncertainty.

"I know what you are thinking Diya, and believe me, I know how it feels. I just couldn't share this with anyone. The moment I realized I have to live with it, my brain froze. I went completely blank. It has been difficult since then, more than I can ever tell," Aadi said shakily.

"I can't believe I never got a hint of things," Diya said with despair.

"Look, we need to know the truth Aadi, no matter how hard it is. The stories we live, the moments we experience, we don't always leave them behind. They become a part of us - a part of who we are," Diya said looking deep into his eyes as if she had all the answers. "Sometimes we are unaware of how things can grow tougher inside. We try speculating things out of the overwhelmed chaos for a better perspective, but something still prevails in the background. I just want you to speak up your mind. We may figure something out," she said convincingly.

"Diya, these days I just sit quietly and do nothing Absolutely nothing. The days are not as they used to be. Something is killing me from inside and I can't figure out what it is. I started seeing Dr. Eva lately and I think she understands my situation," Aadi began to explain anxiously. "My emotions are heightened and intensified all the time. Most part of the day I feel sad, it has all got very confusing. I don't feel good about myself. I only think of things I've done wrong: the relationships I've ruined, commitments I could not honour, the people I disappointed." he continued. "Somewhere I also believe that my heart will fix everything itself but it's my mind I can't control. It makes me worry about the memories I've kept locked up in the quiet corners somewhere around me. Some of them don't belong there. Some of them I've tried so hard forgetting that even the thought of them coming back shakes the hell out of me. I tried to make my peace with it. I just kept the pieces that hurt and I don't even know why. The unforgettable love that is still deeply rooted inside. It cuts through me like shards of glass. It's my mind that keeps me up the whole night, makes me cry, destroys me over and over again. Finally, I convinced my mind to let it go because it already knows how to heal."

Aadi was hurriedly speaking everything, his mind was scrambled. He seemed to be jumping from one topic to another. The velocity at which his thoughts were changing had no limit. His energy was getting drained with the speed of his thoughts.

Later that day, he had a follow-up session with Dr. Eva.

Dr. Eva had some sessions with people who wanted to open up and soften the things that kept them drowning in the darkness of their sorrows. Aadi's confusion and insecurities made him visit her so that he could cope up with his fears and dilemmas.

Aadi started going to those sessions secretly without letting anyone know. He wanted to vocalize everything that was going on in his head. Eva was aware of the fact that he was always nervous while talking to her and that he was still not prepared to open up.

Dr. Eva said concerningly, "Aadi, I know what you are going through. I understand the chaos you are carrying. But trust me, we should have an open talk. Stop fighting yourself and talk. Talk about the thing that is eating you up. Relax and clarify your thoughts. Make sure you take regular doses of prescribed medicines. Believe me, things will fall in place."

Aadi said worryingly, "Sorry Dr. Eva, I respect the efforts you are taking. It's just that I have lost all the hopes. A close friend of mine, Diya, has come here with me today. I discussed all these things with her yesterday. I was going through a turbulent thought process all over again. My mind was just not at peace due to all the random anxiety-laden thoughts in my head. And amidst this, I talked to Diya and found solace while unravelling the thoughts that had made my heart heavy.".

"Diya! You never mentioned anything about her before. Firstly, tell me if you have been taking your medications regularly. Have you? After your last follow-up?" asked the Doctor.

"Medicines? Of course, I take them. I mean I guess I do else Diya would have known about it all this time. To tell you honestly, she has been living with me for the past few weeks. I know I never told you this. It took me some time to share," Aadi muttered "Tell me, would it be terrible on my part to miss any of my dosages?" he asked. "I hate to say this to you and trust me I am very grateful to you for looking out for me all the time but I think the medicines are creating more chaos these days, I couldn't even sleep. It feels like I am blank about what lies ahead in my life, the anxiety has taken a complete toll on me. I was all fine and fully relaxed until last week. I don't know what came over all of a sudden, I felt helpless and worthless. I felt very needy so I called Diya over."

She remembered their last talk over a phone call, so Dr. Eva consoles Aadi, "We are as resilient as we can be, these feelings of helplessness are just momentary. But when these feelings play with your mind... they create havoc and void full of resentments. Our experiences often develop and pile up a mixed bag of emotions that an individual carries throughout his or her life, with different layers of reactions, sentiments, and a lot of going on in the background. Somewhat like every cloud might have a silver lining, but sometimes it is very difficult to realize its significance. Especially when the emotions crash to the ground and create a disturbance all over the place."

Aadi with satisfaction confessed, "Diya made me understand that all these things are merely an illusion of a mishap, and I am just devastated because of all these things bombarding on me suddenly and literally out of nowhere. I am just overthinking and making my own life complicated for no reason. The moments when I am not even able to comprehend, and I am just collapsing into nothingness. But I am not sure, I wish to evolve extensively, outgrow bitter experiences no matter what I am right now. This is what Diya made me believe in, and I still remember the moment how I felt lighter after I got a chance to discuss things with Diya. Then from that moment, I have decided to keep the pieces that make me feel out of the world, away from myself, and think about better things that are there for me to be a better man. Moreover, all left are just the pieces of my old memories that are scattered all over the place. It's only my mind that keeps me alive with the memories that convince me to hold on to them, the memories that make me smile through my tears empowers me over and over again. By the time I will end up living like a normal happy person and something inside me won't eat me alive anymore, I will surely convince my mind to fly like this because it would already know how to deal... And I would be healed for good."

Aadi comprehended and shared a smile. Dr. Eva speculated that Aadi was a bit confident this time as if he could find out his real soul and his life will no more be an enigma.

Dr. Eva with curiosity, "Aadi, Can I meet Diya? Is she with you today?"

Aadi with a golden smile on his face, "Yes Dr. Eva why not. She is just waiting outside."

Dr. Eva and Aadi came out of the cabin to meet Diya. "Diya... Diya..." Aadi was a bit confused.

"Dr. Eva she was just here with me, I came with her here." Aadi panicked.

Dr. Eva now realized that things are a bit far. It crossed the normal course, which is now hanging onto a thin line between reality and a mere illusion. Thinking about Aadi, she recognized how his own life is swirling around enigmas. That is deeper than what it is, the emotions that are so misunderstood and drowning in his reflections which are in that mirror. Mere an image of his alter-ego that always brought up the good in him.

That satisfied your urges, cravings, and calmed you down in your bad times. In the end, everything is what you feel and what you hold back deep down in your heart. The heart that beats for you to pump up the accurate amount of oxygen you need. But the same heart that is overburdened with misconceptions, and the reflections of a person living within you. The reflections overpower the darkness that swallows up the essence of your life. And dumps you into the heap of fallacies.

This keeps him in the middle of a situation where Aadi's sober side knows what his emotions and feelings are, how useless he felt about himself. But that shadow of Diya brightened his life. Nonetheless, had all the magic to cheer him up with her charms. And bring the good in him from all the blackness he had been through.

At times we are so jacked up in our space full of worries that a person like Aadi finds peace with the illusions around him in the virtual world.

3

Relapse

by Karen Pereira

Michael lay on his bed staring up at the ceiling as he had been for the past couple of days. He watched the fan whirling above him, his eyes following the circling blades as the faint noise of the motor calmed him.

Something new. Something different. That might help take off the edge.

He recalled the advice his therapist had given him a week prior. So far, nothing had seemed to draw his fancy. Michael had begun to believe that nothing would make him feel the way he used to. The rush of adrenaline and the particular smell that he equated it with. He was afraid that nothing would pacify him.

A small smile played on his face as he revelled in the feeling. A shiver ran down his spine when he pictured all the things he could do with one tiny instrument. He shut his eyes, revelling in the faint memory from a month ago, the warm sunshine from the open window on his face felt like a new beginning.

However, the good memories also brought back the guilt. The feeling that he had tried to conquer ever since he saw his therapist for the first time.

Michael's eyes snapped open.

Something new to take off the edge.

He continued gazing above him, his absentminded eyes darting all over the ceiling when a small black spot brought his wandering mind back.

Michael's once glazed over eyes now focused on the tiny black spot that disappeared behind the blades for a fraction of a second before returning into his line of sight. The minuscule black spot irked the recumbent man. He sat up; resting his weight on his forearms, his eyes still trained on what seemed like an insignificant spot in his perfect house. His eyebrows furrowed, and his mind raced, wondering how he had never noticed it before.

The lights in the supermarket blinded him as soon as he stepped in through the automatic doors. He hated the bright floodlights that made him lose the sense of time. The supermarket always seemed like a place where reality seemed warped. He shoved his fists into his coat pockets and headed towards the section that held the paints.

He needed something new to take the edge off. The black spot that plagued his ceiling had irked him. The uneasy feeling that enveloped him every time he had turned back had begun to set in. However, this time he was adamant. He strode on, focusing on the soft thud of his boots on the tiled floor, as he clenched his fists tighter to keep them from shaking.

***

Michael was calmer when he stood in line at the checkout counter. His hand was wrapped around the handle of a paint can that best matched the colour of his ceiling and his other hand clasped around the handle of a brush. Michael stared at the young cashier behind the counter. He fixated on the colour of his eyes.

One blue, one green.

The faint beeping from the scanner wafted around him until it faded off. Michael continued to stare at the oddity before him, a small frown gracing his face.

He placed his paint can and brush on the counter, noticing that the person before him had finished. He paid for his things and left. The differently coloured eyes absconded as soon as he stepped out into the warm afternoon.

"How long had it been?"

He thought to himself as he headed over to his car.

Michael felt a little at ease, as he drove back home. He smiled. He was making progress. Some of the weight that he had felt earlier had lifted. The cashier with his differently coloured eyes did not bother him as much as it would have before. All he could think of was the black spot on his ceiling and the coat of paint that would go over it.

His therapist would be very pleased. He could not wait to see him the following week.

Michael pushed the door to his apartment open. He missed the smell that usually greeted him, the faint smell that travelled around with him.

***

Michael walked into his room, a stack of newspapers in his hand and the paint can in another.

It was 7 o'clock, next morning when Michael had finished covering his room with the newspaper. He had spent most of the previous day meticulously covering the floor and pushing his furniture against the walls.

He had decided to sleep on the couch the prior night and he woke up with a crick in his neck. However, throughout the night, as he stared up at the ceiling of his living room and watched the moving lights that mimicked the traffic outside, all he could think about was the spot on the adjacent ceiling.

Michael looked around his black and white room in the overalls that had remained untouched for over a month. His cupboard had been layered with 'The Times' from two weeks ago, and the fan with the most recent one. The headline lay across the blade;

The local cashier goes missing after the afternoon shift at the supermarket.

Michael found it amusing when he had pasted it on like a proclamation. He did not like that man anyway.

Michael had never been fond of the news, it had always painted him in a horrible light, even when he had tried to quit. However, the paper had come in handy in the past as it had now. Layers of it had been a good absorbent. He hated stains on his walls and paper was a cheaper alternative to plastic.

Michael dragged his step ladder under the fan, the spot where his single bed had been. He climbed up the ladder, paint can and brush were in his hand. He set it down on the last rung of the ladder and moved the blade aside.

Michael peered at the unusual bump on his ceiling. It was black and had tiny strands sticking out from it. Michael climbed a little higher. The bump seems clearer now.

Hair.

Hair stuck out as tiny strands from the small bump on his ceiling. Michael paled as he stared at it. His hands shook as memories flashed through the back of his mind. Memories that he had tried hard to suppress.

The dark dank room and the man to whom the mole belonged to. The crunch of plastic tarp under his feet, the black and white newspaper on the wall, the feel of the wooden hilt in his hand as he carved it off his face. Memories of the man's horror-struck face were enough to snap Michael back to reality.

Unlike the previous day, he did not like the familiar feeling that engulfed him. The feeling that he had been working on. He grabbed the brush from the paint can and hurriedly painted over the mole in the wall. He thought he had gotten rid of it, as he had with all the other mementos that he had kept over the years as a reminder of the world he was building. A world without imperfections.

Michael focused on the faint scratching sound of the brush against the plaster as he painted over the spot until he felt that it would not haunt him anymore. The patch on the ceiling standing out against the rest. The trembling man carefully got off the ladder and pulled out his phone. He had to talk to his therapist before things got worse.

"Everything will be okay."

The words played around in Michael's head. The same words that his therapist had explained to him over the phone.

"Everything will be okay."

Michael repeated to himself as he sat in the corner of his room staring at the reflection of a scared man in the mirror. He had lost track of time at some point in his rant, only for his therapist to calmly said,

"Everything will be okay."

Michael backed into the corner as he looked up at the ceiling. The black spot staring back at him again, more prominent than ever. Michael clutched at the paintbrush in his hand and the empty paint can stand next to him. He had painted over the same spot all through the morning, only for it to keep reappearing.

"Everything will be okay."

Michael repeated to himself as he walked out of his room with shaky steps and closed the door behind him. He left his small apartment that afternoon and did not return until nightfall. He stood outside his therapist's office the whole time. Repeating the same words over and over again until he began to believe them himself.

When Michael walked back into his room that night, the mole was gone, leaving behind spots of paint. Michael let out a sigh of relief; however, he slept on the couch that night.

***

Sunlight streamed through Michael's open windows, hitting his face. His eyes fluttered open and he sat up groggily. He ran his hands over his face and through his hair, dishevelling it, the events from the previous day rushing through his mind. He got off the couch and headed to his room. He looked up at the clear ceiling and sighed in relief. The mole had disappeared. Covered under the layers of paint he presumed.

However, the relief did not last for very long, for as he walked into his kitchen and pulled open his refrigerator door, his face grew pale. He stared inside for a while until the consistent beeping snapped him out of his daze. He slowly shut the door with trembling hands and left his apartment.

Michael drove to the therapist's office again. At least what the man called an office located in a warehouse half a mile out from the small town.

*****

Michael was calm when he sat in the chair that faced his therapist. Calmer than he had ever been. A strange smile played on his face as he waited for the other person to say something. When he did not, Michael took it upon himself to break the silence that engulfed them.

"When I woke up this morning doctor, I was sure I had left what I considered the worst part of myself behind. The mole was gone, however, the constant anxiousness remained." He paused, hoping the man would say something.

"However, when I opened my refrigerator only to find it staring back at me, all of those conflicted feelings rushed back. I had never been more scared. A feeling that had always eluded me. I was sure I was going insane. But as I drove here, it dawned on me." He continued, staring at the man.

"This therapy. What you convinced me to go through was not because you wanted me to quit. It was to make me realize how good I had it. You wanted me to abstain so that when I finally got back to it, I won't let the newspapers affect me the way they did. So that I wouldn't have to doubt myself."

Michael paused as he sat in the cushioned chair in front of a full-length mirror.

The strange smile had widened as he glanced towards the door next to it and the rest of the man that was strapped to a chair in it. Michael found it easier when his victims were awake. However, he had gotten rid of the flashy uniform that the cashier had worn.

"You see doctor, I should have realized what you were up to ever since I saw the two differently coloured eyes in my refrigerator. How you got it there still amazes me."

A rattling sound from the room drew his attention. He was awake.

"Well. I think this is the last I will be seeing you, doctor. At least for now." He said as he got off the chair and headed towards the room.

He pushed the door open and looked back into the full-length mirror.

"You were right.

Everything will be okay."

4

Sapphire

by Rosalind Reshma

An eerie silence surrounds me and I find comfort in its familiarity. This is my favourite hour of the day. Night, to be accurate. I like watching the sleeping world. Vulnerable and oblivious to the dangers lurking in the dark. I like this ritual of aloneness that I get to enjoy every night. The aloneness and the cigarettes. I take out another cigarette from the almost empty packet, carefully, not to crumble the perfection of the shiny paper, and light it before giving it the company of my trembling lips.

"It doesn't matter," I tell myself. "Five years is a long time. It's time to let go."

I take a puff, hold the smoke, and let the taste fill my mouth.

Manav admiring my blue eyes while discussing politics and us... A lifetime ago. Kisses, moonlight coloured, golden rum-flavoured.

I release the smoke and memory. I watch it fade as it moves towards the starry sky. I hold another memory.

Chicken soup from a plastic bowl. The furry blanket around me. Manav's voice assures me that I'll get better.

Release. Let it fade.

Manav reading out Shelley. Warmth seeping through the remnants of rain on his shirt, onto my cold cheek.

Let it go.

The glittery wedding and promises of a happily ever after.

I am dragged back to reality by a sudden touch of heat. I have finished the cigarette. I loosen my grip and see the glowing dot fly from my balcony on the fifth floor. I wait for it to touch the ground and disappear into the darkness before grabbing the next.

Broken coffee mugs. Hurtful words. Long silences.

I accidentally swallow the smoke. I try to cough it out. It burns my eyes and throat. I never get to see this memory fade into the vast sky. It always ends up dissolving in me. I take the next puff.

Locked refrigerator. The feel of hot oil against the skin. The smell of burning hair. The coldness of the razor sliding on the back of my neck.

The wind takes the smoke away from me. I am satisfied.

The deafening silence, sirens, and my voice telling the police that it was not an accident... My voice screamed that my husband was murdered by a little girl in a blue dress... Shrugs of disbelief and pity.

I let the smoke go and watch it as it slowly fades. Suddenly, the silence is broken by a group of street dogs. Suddenly, my hour of aloneness is snatched away. I look down, annoyed. Between their loud barks, I notice a feeble cry. After a few minutes, the silence is restored. I am about to get back to the task of shedding memories when I hear a knock. My first thought is to ignore it. Three in the morning is not an appropriate time to bother anyone. The knock continues. Irritated, I step back into the detested house and walk through the ghosts of the past, towards the door. I open it to see a frail woman. Teary-eyed.

"Hi." She begins nervously. "I'm extremely sorry about this. But do you have a spade?"

"Spade?" It comes out harsher than I intended it to.

"Y-yes... A spade." She's scared but not willing to give up. "Or anything I can dig the ground with."

"Dig the ground? Why do you want to do that at this unearthly hour?" I am curious.

"Please, it's urgent." Something in her voice moves me.

"Okay. Wait here." I tell her and go to the kitchen to find something.

I don't want to be in the kitchen. It scares me. I grab the first thing I see and rush out.

"Here," I tell her, handing her the long-perforated steel ladle. "I don't have a spade, but I hope this will do."

"Thank you." She says, taking it from me and I know that she means it. And I feel guilty for some reason.

"I'll come with you." I offer, surprising myself.

"Thank you so much. I could do it with some help..." She smiles at me through the tears.

When we are in the lift, I notice that she's carrying a shoebox. I look up at her and our eyes meet.

"A kitten was killed some time ago." She explains. "By a bunch of dogs... I couldn't save it. By the time I ran down and chased the dogs away, it was too late. The kitten was barely alive. I want to bury it. Don't want the little thing to be mutilated again."

I'm touched by her kindness and ashamed of my indifference to the world around me. I was busy smoking and dwelling in the past while a helpless animal was being ruthlessly murdered. This wasn't who I was. Where and when did that kind-hearted and brave person die and give birth to this uncaring and whiny woman?

We walk across the lawn quietly. She kneels beside a newly planted sapling. The soil around it is still loose and wet. I stand there watching her. She briefly opens the shoe box and gently strokes the dead kitten. I turn away. I don't want to see it. I can't. I look at her when I hear the steel touching the ground.

"Why did they kill it?" She is talking to no one in particular. "It was such a small and helpless thing! If it were something they could eat, I wouldn't have felt so sad about it. But what is the point of killing or hurting something with no purpose... Just for the sake of killing..."

And she breaks down. And then I notice it. The ferocity with which her hands are moving. As if she's hurting the world by digging it hard. Hurting it for all the pain the helpless and the weak suffer in the hands of their oppressors. Trying to make things right. For the kitten. For herself... I kneel beside her and place a hand on her shoulder.

"How old were you?" I ask.

She stops digging. Looks at me with an expression I can't fathom.

"Nine." She replies and resumes digging. A little less urgently.

"Who was it?" I can't stop myself from asking.

"It was my father's friend. His daughter used to be a good friend of mine." She tells me. There is a brief silence and for some reason, I give this unknown girl a face and a voice.

"It was two days before my birthday." She resumes. "My parents decided to plan a surprise party. Told me they are going to visit a doctor, but I knew they were going to the town. To buy me the electric train set I had asked for. I pretended that I believed them and waved them goodbye. Little did I know that after that day no toy train can make me happy. I was left with that monster..."

"What about his wife... And the daughter?" I'm hoping that she'd tell me it was an instance of attempted sexual abuse.

"His wife was at her mother's place. The daughter had gone for tuition... I realized that something bad was happening only when it started hurting me."

She stops talking and places the shoebox in the hole she has made. She looks at it for about a minute and then starts burying it.

"It's funny." She resumes. "That day I cried because my favourite frock was torn. It was a beautiful one. Sapphire blue, like your eyes, with frills and sequins."

There is a brief pause.

"All of us live with our past." She tells me with a sigh. "All of us allow it to shape our future. But some of us know how to shrug the past. I think that is who I am... That is who I believe I am. But there are days when I still cry for my sapphire blue frock."

She laughs and gets up.

"I'll wash your ladle..." She begins.

"It's okay," I tell her and grab the ladle back. "It's just mud."

She doesn't protest. We are silent till the door of the lift opens. She thanks me again before we part and apologizes for the trouble. I tell her that it's okay.

The past cannot be shrugged off. If it could be, I wouldn't be having the same nightmare years after I lost a loved one... One in which he is begging me to not do it and I push him down an abyss with a hatred that could have easily been centuries old. I know that I am not that person even though sometimes it is too eloquent to be a dream... So eloquent that it almost seems like a memory... I brush away the thought. It was an accident. There was no little girl. That's what everybody had told me. That's what I have been telling myself.

The past stays dormant, deep inside, waiting for a familiar smell, taste, a forgotten song, a dead kitten, or a lonely night to trigger the turbulence of memories or nightmares of memories that could have been.

I am drowning and have no control over it... I am slipping into oblivion, my heart shattered into a million painful shards, and beside me the emptiness... I am trying to vanish in my puff again... I am crying, the tears flowing with a will of their own, leaving little dark patches on a torn sapphire blue frock. I can see a silver sequin on the floor and try to pick it up, but I cannot move. I am frozen...

We all have stories looming over us... Stories that cannot be revealed, past that, have scarred us. A catastrophe that allows us to absorb the pitch-black darkness. The darkness that pushes us over the edge all over again no matter how much we want to fade away into nothingness. Even when everything is blurry, I am haunted by the nine-year-old in the blue frock.

I catch a glimpse of my eyes on the surface of the muddy ladle and for a brief moment, I catch a glimpse of hatred lurking behind the sapphire blue.

It wasn't me. I assure myself and walk on.

5

Of Memories and Pain

by Anamika Kundu

Beautiful fall day. The sun was streaming through the colourful red, gold, and orange leaves of the tree-lined drive up to the school. Children and adults could be heard yelling, "Bye!"

"Love you!"

"Have a good day!"

As Ronnie jogged up the last few steps, he was smiling cause his Dad had promised to take him camping this evening. They, just the boys; would pitch up a tent on the hillside, barbeque hotdogs on a real log fire, and later watch the stars. Fantastic!

Bang!

Bang! Bang!

As he turned around, he was surprised to see a young man with a gun firing at all the people around.

"What's wrong with him?" Then he felt something warm in his stomach as he collapsed, right at the door.

Jonathan couldn't believe his ears when he received the call from the school. He called Janet and they raced the car, on their way to the school. The drive was lined with parents, teachers, and students. Grief lay like a warm blanket! Forcing the people to come closer to grapple with this shocking and pointless death of young children and Ms. Sandy, one of the more popular teachers.

Jonathan kept sitting in the garden, it was quite late and Janet was worried about him. With their young son gone, the future had come crashing down like waves at the shore. She was not going to lose her husband if she could help it. "Honey! Come let's pray before dinner." He didn't seem to hear. She gently held him by the hand and led him into the house.

Time is a great healer they say, and as days went past Jonathan and Janet held on to each other, sifting through Ronnie's belongings and reliving precious moments. Their friends came around now and then as did the neighbours for they were well-loved and respected.

Jonathan was a veteran having been on several tours where he forged great bonds with fellow soldiers.

He was also known as 'Bullseye' as he always struck bullseye when he fired his gun. He had seen a lot of deaths and seen life up close. But he never imagined his life without his son. A fine boy; gentle, caring, and great at sports. What a meaningless way to lose a life filled with promise. Having great faith, he resolved to work hard so that no more lives would be lost, to the free access to guns.

Janet was a housewife who loved to paint. She would teach painting over the weekends to children and housewives. Her work was much appreciated in her neighbourhood, among friends, and in the local club. Ronnie was convincing her to put up an exhibition. Her caring and loving nature endeared her to one and all. She had been on her own while her husband would be gone for long stretches, she ensured she always responded to any need for help in her community.

She was passing by the big hardware store when she saw a woman being accosted by a few teenagers. She swung her car into the park, without pausing, even as she called 911.

One of the boys turned towards her and she asked, "What's up boys?"

Stunned, she looked at them, "Put the gun away!"

One of them shot her.

She barely whispered before collapsing to the ground...

The boys yanked the other woman's purse and ran away as fast as they could...

The woman ran to the store to call for help. The Police were already there, wheeling Janet to the Emergency, en route she left to be with Ronnie. Jonathan was like a wild animal.

For days he grieved in silence. His friends and neighbours did as much as they could. He seemed to have withdrawn. Victor arrived then.

He ensured meals were cooked, the house was cleaned, and even told Jonathan to "snap out of it!"

One day he announced he was going to take revenge.

On his walks around town, if he noted someone happy and smiling, he would discreetly follow them, check out their whereabouts, and if feasible, plan to end their lives. Just like Ronnie and Janet had been taken away! For no rhyme or reason.

A lady out shopping was found dead in the car park. There seemed to be no clues, no motive, and no suspect. People were curious and the police were furious. A few days later, a man out for a run in the park was found shot dead by the park rangers. This was getting too much. Simple, happy people seemed to be shot for no reason.

Victor laughed when he read the reports in various newspapers. "See, I have avenged you!"

Jonathan was slowly limping back to some sort of normalcy. With his happy family wiped out in days, there was nothing normal left for him. He couldn't understand what Victor was talking about. He threw himself into his crusade against easy access to guns, one way to end pointless killings and deaths.

The human mind is the strongest tool we have or the most potent enemy. In between, there are so many roles it plays and so many tasks it completes either known to us or unknown, deep in our subconscious. As we go about our daily routine, it's up to us to give in to our mind and play the victim or collect our senses and motivate ourselves to rise above any calamity. Our beliefs and our faith help us to make the choice.

Victor would taunt Jonathan often for being unable to lash out at those who cruelly had snatched his beloved family and left him devastated. Jonathan being an easy-going person took no heed of this new entrant in his life. Victor, on the other hand, being dominating and aggressive, took it on himself to protect his softer brethren.

One day, Mrs. Jacobson, Jonathan's neighbour hurried across the street on seeing him, but she was nonplussed as he simply walked past her. No greeting, no recognition, not even a smile. Her heart went out to the poor man, nobody should have to deal with such calamity.

She mentioned it to her husband after dinner. Now Police officer Jacobson thought it outright strange. He was well aware of Jonathan's gentlemanly demeanour and found it difficult to believe that a man could change so much. "Darling was there anything else that was different?" He asked.

"Hmm... Now that you ask me, yes, he seemed more confident. And walked far more briskly, rather jauntily than I have ever seen him do before. He had a strange look in his eye too, a rather distant preoccupation."

The next day at the Police station, he sent for Officer Timothy Branson. He wanted him to follow up a few investigations regarding the recent murders in town including that of Janet. Coincidentally the TV was telecasting an interview with Jonathan, just then. He was appealing to the government to impose strict regulations to curb access to arms. He had collected signatures from parents, teachers, elderly people, college students, and even a few retired folks. Hmm... Some people could turn their tragedy into something good for society.

Officer Branson in due course of his investigation came up with the number plate of a car which was seen in both the places of murder. It came upon the Security camera footage. On checking the registration, it was found to belong to Mr. Jonathan, and the address was given. What a strange coincidence! He decided to go and meet up with Jonathan. When he knocked at the door, he heard a distinct "Come in." He walked in

"Hello, Officer! How can I help you?"

"Hello, Sir! I am Officer Timothy Branson, I just wanted to know a few things about Mrs. Janet." "Oh! I am Victor. I am sorry I don't know anything about her. You should ask about this to Jonathan. And he is out of town for a few days."

"When did he leave sir?"

"He left a week ago. He needed a change of scenery. Atleast, that's what he said to me."

"I will come around after taking an appointment later, then."

At the station, he reported the conversation to Officer Jacobson. He was taken aback. Jonathan was on Television right now and his wife had seen him the previous evening.

"That's the guy Victor! So much like Jonathan... Yet, somehow different! More arrogant!" Said Branson as he pointed to the TV.

Jacobson's senses were zinging. He took Branson and went over to Jonathan's house immediately. On knocking at the door, there was no response. He knocked again... Persistently. They heard footsteps coming down the stairs. The door opened. There was Jonathan! "Hello! How can I help you, officer?"

"Hello, Jonathan!"

"I am Victor!"

Officer Jacobson was stunned. Something downright fishy here. Why was Jonathan calling himself Victor? He instantly recalled all that his wife had told him. He looked at Branson and signalled to record their conversation discreetly.

"Hello, Victor! I am Officer Jacobson, and I think you have already met Officer Timothy Branson. Can we come in?"

After hesitating for just that slight moment too long, he moved aside and let them in.

"I have just a few questions for you, we won't take too much time."

"Ok!"

"When did you arrive here?"

"The day after Janet passed away, you know, Jonathan's wife. He was weeping like a helpless child. To think he is a veteran, much respected in his regiment by everyone. You know he is called Bullseye? I couldn't take his pitiful state and so I had to come. If I had been around earlier, both Ronnie and Janet would have been alive. But someone will have to pay," he muttered.

"Excuse me, what do you mean by that?"

"Hmm, nothing."

"Jonathan is so engrossed in his campaign to ban sales of arms to common people. What do you think?" Asked Jacobson.

"I don't think anything will come out of that! And in any case, he won't get his family back, will he?" Shouted Victor.

His eyes were spewing fire and there was a wild look about him.

"Ok! Could you tell me where you were before you came here?"

"Ah... Ah... I was in New York! It's a big city you know!"

"Hmm. Surely. Do you have your ID? May I see it?"

He fumbled in his pockets, desperately looking for his wallet, and said, "Actually I lost my wallet and my driving license with it, officer!"

"In that case will you please come to the police station with us? We can help you."

As they were moving out of the room... Victor lunged at Jacobson in a bid to take his pistol. But the officer was far too quick for him. He somersaulted and neatly pinned Victor down.

Branson cocked his pistol then, pointing it straight at Jonathan, "Your game is over, put your hands up."

It was a highly engrossing lawsuit, State versus Veteran, with people all agog. There was sympathy and admiration for him. The law took its course as the Defense lawyer proved Jonathan had absolutely nothing to do with it... Victor had!

6

Balance

by Prajitha Ravipati

S mall towns with hills around covered with green beds and with blue blankets. A happy place with families living a peaceful and stress-free life was an odd and orthodox family out of all this even energy. They took pride in their culture and in perfecting religious rituals and traditions, on that money mattered.

There was no room for mistakes. Grinding themselves and their kids to be perfect. In all this, the youngest of the family who was friendly, slow learner, confused, non-sorted, believer of modern thinking Kanya was being crushed and her elder brother a fun-loving, sorted, smart, caring, and adaptable person Raman was her best friend, support, and strength, standing by her side all the time and being there in toughest times and as a guru taught her. On the journey of designing their children as an idol model of the caste used physical abuse as their tool more than love, kids never felt at home, it was a battlefield, always battling against their emotions. Apart from all this, parents were not happy. A pressure on them to fulfil the debts hustled twenty-four hours, pressure on kids to help in business, facing torture daily. She wasn't able to take all this. Though Raman was on her side and slowly, depression has taken over her, and she became a victim of depression.

The only choice Kanya's brain had to escape from the situation was adapting a defensive mechanism and this had brought an unexpected turn in Kanya's life. She acted completely like a different person, sometimes her actions, the posture of her body, and the way she was addressing people and disturbing their normal life was not her still.

Brother was amazed to watch the way she was chanting, later he asked, "How did you do that? You were amazing!"

Kanya replied, "Did I?" In surprise. Sounding unsure of what he was talking about, said thank you! Many more unusual incidents happened. She was doing her homework and household work without any help and gained knowledge in culture, customs, traditions, and been performing rituals perfectly.

Later, Raman became suspicious of her unusual behaviour and even noticed the level of her health and mental stability were falling. He was prepared to take her to the hospital but an unbelieving incident happened before that.

Raman's death.

With this, her unstable composure was completely broken down a veil of discomposure covered her face, stayed, and continued.

A decade passed; Kanya was a 25-years-old young woman who was living a separate life, away from family and was on the journey of finding herself. To start it, she surveyed a few part-time jobs. She went for the first location... The interviewer got impressed and selected her.

Her face turned completely blank, she was not understanding what he was talking about. She returned and narrated the whole story to Rose, a friend at the hostel. Who had a fair idea of what was happening with her? She consoled her.

In the evening that day, Rose starts telling her what happened from the day Kanya came here. While Rose was caught up in the unfolding of this mysterious life Kanya had, on the other side Kanya was sweating over and stress was building up deep inside and was about to burst out with fear that's when Ram confronts Kanya, he asked her to tell Rose a different story the actual one where she isn't the victim. Where the job interview taught her and gave her hope.

Ram is 27 years old, he took care of her since she lost her brother. The phase when she lost her composure, being in a dissociated state, living like a dead person, Ram was the only one to protect her from the emotional burden that she felt, he endured the pain she felt.

The way Ram contradicted the story... Kanya and Rose both were convinced to look at the story from a different perspective. He goes out for a walk, and he saw an advertisement for an audition for singing... He thought that he got freedom and could follow his passion.

The next morning, Kanya woke up with a headache and tried remembering what happened, meanwhile she got a call from her office. The call triggered her... But she always had a neighbour, the one who was as soothing as Ram is.

Luv's support and care calmed her, and she had an amazing conversation with the interviewer. Kanya starts with a good beginning on a new journey.

Luv knew Kanya since she was a little girl. They grew up together and their bond has been inseparable since then. She stood by her side when Kanya stopped functioning because of the emotional and physical abuse she faced from her parents and never received the love, attention, and encouragement that Kanya always wanted except for her brother and Luv.

Luv is a 26-year-old girl, an old soul, a genius, and she had a keen interest in mythology.

Headache is not leaving her, even the dizziness and voices came up in support for levelling her pain. Two streets away, her favourite coffee house was calling to heal! Kanya couldn't resist so she left. Having a coffee sip by sip brought calmness but still... Her thought process was not able to express herself. Something happens and took a tissue and wrote a note:

'I came here to find myself, instead, I am lost. Day by day memory is fading, frequency of health is so fallen I don't feel young anymore, the heart feels so sick, and the brain is acting like an alien. What is happening to me? Feels like a shadow is always following me and not abandoning my side, no matter what I am doing from me being at rest time, in dreams, and even in my thoughts making life like hell, it has occupied a permanent space in my mind and my heart listens to the same voices again and again and again. "You need us" repeatedly and loudly. "We are you and we are all one" louder than before.'

She bursts out in anger. Took a cab. She slips into the music as the driver plays his favourite music singing all over the way till she reaches the hostel. The cab driver puts a weird expression while Kanya was paying him. She felt relaxed and light... Yet not healed, still concerned about her health issues, she decided to have a check-up.

She was prescribed some medicines now.

She kept using medicines and maintained a journal, meanwhile, these two were in a discussion that Luv has enrolled in a course of three months. Ram wanted to give auditions, he has been waiting for a very long time to get the freedom finally, he had fixed his schedule accordingly, soon they were indulged in their personal life.

Kanya was reliving her depression phase all over again. Ram takes over the critical situation and soothes her with music, while he was playing music, he found a journal she maintained. There were small notes in the journal about the issues she faced about the voices she heard, the society cornering her, and not accepting her. He realized that all these days she has been so self-observant that he has forgotten about his prime duty and responsibility for taking care of Kanya.

Kanya has found the notes left by Ram and Luv.

Ram said, "I am like your brother, and being with you for so long is a wonderful journey and will always be."

Luv's note saying, "Hi my Girl we don't know each other that deeply but, I knew since you were a child. I love doing all your work and even now."

Those notes scared the daylight out of her and the soul became scared still of the unknown, for no specific reason. She was knitting her thoughts, standing still, till the thoughts stopped pricking her heart. She became numb... Sections of her brain cleared their paths.

She read those notes twice or thrice again...

Kanya mumbles, "Are they a part of me?"

Her best friend replied, "Maybe yes or maybe no. Arghh! I don't know... Where are they and why can't I meet them."

Kanya said furiously, "You cannot meet them... They are shy..."

At this chaotic portion of Kanya's life, Luv and Ram became much more protective, began to pamper, and helped her in all small things. They were spoon-feeding her with loads of stuff instead of helping her out and showing her the right path, the one of study and a probable future job. Ram being the primary protector instead of teaching self-defence, inculcating courage, and making her stronger in situations, became a door to escape from the situations whenever she wanted... He was Kanya's saviour and she found peace behind her shield "Ram and Luv."

Kanya now had faith that whatever happens, she got their back, trusting them blindly and the confidence she had in them instead of gaining her self-confidence.

Ram and Luv whispered together, "We are the voices and feelings that push you off the cliff filled with guilt. We are here for you to remember all the troubles that we have forced you to recollect. You thought we are a version that was born to save you from the pressures and sorrows. But we pushed you into the land of nothingness."

She nurtured parasites that ignited the darkness and sadness she had in her life. The phase where she re-lived the portions of her life she never wanted to experience. Still, she had to live with those reminders that life can't be a piece of cake. And there always is a portion of you that is hollow, that can never fill the misery you have been through into a tiny place of happiness. Just like a naked corpse that can neither be alive nor be forgotten.

7

Reflection

by Vaibhav Koktare

The sky grew darker, painted in a blue hue, one stroke at night and full moon often showed their presence from the slow floating clouds. The fragrance of jasmine was lingering around. She was in huff and puff, panting and drenched in sweat. On the left side of her forehead, there was a bruise and a crimson stream of blood was tripping down on her face. She could barely see anything in this moonlight. The streets that seemed to be pleasing in the day now have turned into something furious and scary!!!

After the long run, the trees became scarce and she landed herself into an open field. Turning behind she noticed that no one was following her anymore. With a parched throat and sore legs, she took a deep breath and started walking. A glimpse of light was visible at a distance. On approaching there, it appeared like a farmhouse as there was no sign of any resident. This vintage piece of the 90's stands tall and well maintained. On the right side, she saw a doorbell and without any hesitation, she rang the bell... Once... Twice... Thrice... Exhausted and restless, her heartbeats started throbbing. She was calming herself down, she tried once again and heard the footsteps approaching...

It was an old lady in her late 50's with expressive eyes like that of an owl and a tiny nose pin on the left side of her sharp-pointed nose, lips flattered with wrinkles around the cheek and long plaited hair touching her waist. She opened the door and was stunned to see Gauri in front of her.

"What happened Beta? You're injured, come inside quickly."

Gauri then followed the old lady and went inside. It was a huge house with a spacious living room, there was a sofa to the left and a dining table in front of her. Windows were covered with pink and sky-blue curtains. Kamlabai told her to sit down on the sofa and went to the kitchen. On the wall, Gauri noticed a black and white picture of a couple holding a small girl and she kept gazing at it. Then she recollected a similar picture of her with her parents but her chain of thoughts was broken by Kamlabai's footsteps. In a tray, she brought her a glass of water, cotton, and turmeric powder to clean her wound. Gauri finished the glass of water within seconds and asked for another one. Kamlabai refilled the glass and handed it to Gauri. Then she started cleaning the wound and applied some turmeric to it. While doing so, she asked, "Beta, what is your name? How are you so badly injured?"

She said, "My name is Gauri, I came here for a vacation. Some goons tried to snatch my purse. I tried saving myself from this situation, and I entered the woods, landed myself here."

She pleaded, "Aunty, can I please stay here for tonight?"

With the softest smile aunty said, "Of course Beta, you can stay upstairs in my daughter's room. I'll clean the room for you, by that time you relax here. I'll give you a call when the dinner is ready and by then my husband will also be back."

After cleaning she called Gauri,

"Come upstairs I will show you the room."

(They started walking towards stairs)

The staircase was curved and semi-circular. Upstairs, there were two rooms. One was of her daughter and on the opposite side, there was a storeroom. Kamlabai showed her room and went downstairs to prepare the meal. Gauri stepped inside the room, it was big and spacious. There was a medium size bed on the right corner of the room covered with a light pink bedsheet, soft cushions on it. Gauri closed the door and switched on the ceiling fan. Then she opened the French window which was exactly opposite to the door and allowed the cold breeze to calm her down. On her left side, there was a dressing table, she went there took a deep breath, and observed herself. Gauri had straight and silky hair up to her shoulder, her curved and thick eyebrows made her black eyes more attractive and on top of that she had cat-eye specs. Her straight nose and plump rosy lips along with a dimple on her left cheek that embraced her beauty. Her wheatish complexion indeed made her more beautiful. The white T-shirt and a blue-colored Denim was a perfect choice on a feminine body like that of hers.

A well-furnished bookshelf was placed near the door. There were books of different genres like suspense, horror, thriller, and much more. It looked like Kamlabai's daughter was a keen reader. Above the bookshelf, on the wall, there was a painting... It was Kamlabai's daughter. Gauri and her age were almost similar. She was looking gorgeous in Royal Blue Nauwari with a Black Shawl having a golden border draped on it. Her wheaty complexion and dimple on the right cheek, eyes like a pitch-black pool on new moon night, having broad forehead with the soft descending ringlets, her thick long braid up to her waist just like a black king cobra. Gauri lost herself in that painting within a moment.

"Gauri! Dinner is ready Beta." Kamlabai said in a loud voice that will be audible to her.

Gauri regained consciousness and came downstairs within a few minutes. It was around 9:30 p.m. on the table Kamlabai introduced her husband to Gauri. He is a former Army officer and was currently involved in his friend's Dairy Business. He complimented Gauri that, if his daughter Mohini was alive today she would be just like her. The dinner was over and Kamlabai asked Gauri to rest. She nodded and went upstairs. Gauri was impressed with Mohini's collection, as she was a keen reader. She picked up a book and decided to read something before going to bed. The book had a brown cover with a layer of dust settled on it, as it remained untouched after Mohini's demise. She wiped off the dust with her hand and opened the book. Turning the pages one by one she found a folded letter. Keeping the book aside she began to read the letter...

"If anyone is reading this, then I'm not alive anymore. My stepmother Kamlabai and her lover have locked me in this room for one month. That witch married my dad for his wealth and property. When she came to know about my Dad's will, in which he wrote, 'If anything happens to me in future then, all my wealth and property should be immediately transferred on my daughter's name i.e. MOHINI SHASHIKANT PARANJAPE.' Then she merely had any interest in him. As of now, he was of no use to them, they decided to kill him and presented it as a car accident. After Dad, I was their next target; they tried all possible ways and means to get my signature on the property papers but failed. Now here I am in this room ALL

ALONE. It seems like I have to take this tough decision, please forgive me, Daddy. Your princess will soon be with you...

I still have faith."

-Mohini

Gauri lost her senses after reading the letter. She went in front of the mirror and looked at herself, imagining how much Mohini would have suffered here. Her heartbeats were throbbing, she could feel the boiling blood and started sweating. She looked at the painting and herself again and again and suddenly BOOM!!! The bulb above the dressing table burst out. In the dark, she managed to find a torch and when she took a glimpse of herself in the mirror, she was wearing the Royal Blue Nauwari and a Black Shawl with a golden border draped on it as if she was MOHINI...

The next morning

Gauri was in tremendous shock as she found herself lying down in the kitchen with a knife in her hand and bloodshed everywhere. There were stains on her white T-shirt. She stood up, her eyes bulged with fear, and her body became cold and numb. Everything was in mess. Kamlabai's body was lying in front of her, there were multiple stabbed wounds on her body. Running away from the kitchen when she entered the hall and found another dead body covered in blood and was wounded, it was Kamlabai's husband. Her face turned pale, she freaked out as she could barely remember anything about last night. Without wasting a moment, she wiped off her fingerprints with a kitchen cloth, washed the knife and hands in the sink, and left that house immediately. She had committed double homicide. In cold-blood without any remorse, and was running like a whirlwind. She ran with all her strength until the house would disappear from her eyesight. All of a sudden, she was on the National Highway, so lost in her thoughts and fear that she couldn't hear the horn and suddenly a truck came and hit her. Her body was thrown away on the other side of the highway and within a fraction of a second Gauri was no more.

Gauri was an emotional child, as her father did the same thing to her mother just like Kamlabai to satisfy his greed for money. Mohini's letter gave a flashback to Gauri's childhood grief.

There was nothing similar in that Royal Blue Nauwari and a Black Shawl with a golden border and her White T-shirt, nonetheless who and how Gauri was killed is still a mystery. Was she the one who wrote that letter? Or just a girl who flipped her switch, blacked-out, and killed two people? Maybe she was just living deep under the layers of secrets that are still untapped. Seriously! Was she? Can she ever give us the answers that others are looking for?

8

Black And White

by Kanchan Hiranandani

It was a Friday night Akash decided to go for a late-night movie with his wife Archana, and their only daughter Mira. After the movie, Mira requested an ice-cream. There was no ice-cream parlour nearby. They have already booked a cab from that location so he told Archana to stay there while he checks for any ice-cream vendor nearby. She told him to come back soon as the cab was about to reach.

"Don't worry I will be back soon." He said.

"Have you seen any ice-cream vendor?" He asked the stranger.

"Walk straight and then turn left to the corner you will find him." He guided.

"Three chocolate ice-creams." He said.

A sudden screech of a vehicle made him turn. He saw a car hit a man crossing the road. He ran after the car but it disappeared. He memorized the number. He came back and examined him and found him dead. As few people gathered around the spot, he left as his family was waiting for him.

"Where is my ice-cream dad?" Mira asked.

"Ice-cream!!!" He asked dumbfounded.

"Oh!!!! Sorry, it fell on my way..." He replied.

"Are you ok?" Archana asked.

"Yes!" Let's go, the cab is here." He said.

When they reached home and Mira slept.

Archana asked, "What is the matter, why are you so worried?"

He narrated the incident and confirmed that he will go to the police station tomorrow morning and will not leave him in any circumstances.

He went to the police station and the police assured him that they will find the owner of the car soon. The next day, his phone rang.

"Come to the police station we have found the owner." The inspector said.

Within half an hour he reached there. Along with the police, they went to the owner's house, and he recognized the car parked outside.

It ensured him that they had reached the right place. The car was not parked properly and it seemed that someone had kept it in a hurry. they rang the bell; an old man opened the door.

"How can I help you, what brings you here?" He asked

"Yesterday who was driving the car parked outside?" The police officer inquired.

"My son but what happened?" He asked.

"Your son has hit the person and ran away from there." He answered.

"What!!!! It can't be possible..." He panicked.

Peter entered and was surprised to see the police in his home. He could not gather his senses and was hit by the wall.

"Where were you last night?" The inspector asked.

"I went to a party at my friend's place yesterday, what happened, sir?" He answered.

"Did you hit someone?" He asked.

He panicked and tried to run away but they caught him and took him to the police station. They started their investigation, found him guilty and put him in jail.

"You can now go Mr. Akash; we will inquire more about this case. you have to come to court as an eyewitness." The officer said.

As he reached home, he found that the old man was standing outside his house.

"What are you doing here?" Akash inquired.

"Please forgive my son, he is innocent." The old man requested.

"No, he is not, the person died... On the spot was innocent." He stormed at him.

The shreds of evidence proved that he has killed the person and a court hearing was scheduled after a week.

His father was very worried and couldn't understand what to do. He went to the police station and requested to save his son. Inspector told him to meet Akash, as he is the only one who can save him from this fuss.

He went to his house and requested him to pull off his complaint but Akash never listened to him.

He was disheartened and he left his house. As he reached the main entrance. The police van appeared.

"Sir, please help me..." The old man requested.

We have found some evidence in this case.

"What!!!" The old man was stunned.

"Yes Mr. Samuel, we will investigate this matter in detail. Akash can only guide us in this."

Police went inside the house.

"How can I help you, sir?" Akash said.

"Nothing much. I just wanted to ask a few questions." The inspector said.

"Was there any other person nearby during the accident?" He interrogated.

"Sir, I told you a hundred times, there was no one around, as it was a late night." He insisted.

"But you told me that you went to buy an ice-cream." He inquired.

"Oh yes!!! I went there looking for an ice-cream vendor but he ran after the accident happened to escape investigation." He said.

"That means you were the only one with the victim?" The officer asked suspiciously.

"For a while but after a few minutes, people gathered around and I left that place as my family was waiting for me." He replied.

Inspector was not satisfied with his answers and thought to interrogate his wife for further investigation. So the next day he went to his wife's office. They called her in the café.

"We have found certain evidence and need to investigate the hit and run case." He said.

"How can I help you, sir?" She said.

"We would like to know about your husband." He insisted.

She hesitantly refused to answer there. So she was told to come to the police station the next day.

She went to the police station the next day. She never visited the police station ever before. She waited for half an hour for the inspector. Questions were pouring into her mind. Suddenly someone called her name and asked her to go to the cabin. She glances around the room.

They started questioning Akash's behaviour.

"He is a good person and remains calm!" She retorted.

We have inquired from your neighbour. They complained that he is aggressive and violent sometimes and one day during a fight he tried to kill someone. His voice also changes when he is violent.

She was anxious now and thought of speaking the truth.

"Sometimes his behaviour is upside down. He becomes violent. He had a bad childhood. He used to love his grandfather a lot but he was a cruel landlord. He lends money to people and charges a high rate of interest and when they can't return it on time, he forcefully takes their land. One day villagers made a plan to kill him. Akash and his grandfather went to attend a marriage function in a nearby village. On the way back villagers gathered around and killed him brutally they even hit him even after he died. This made a great impact on Akash's mind."

"This is all?" He inquired.

"Yes, sir..." She said.

The post-mortem report says that the victim was not killed on the spot. He was killed brutally afterward.

"Will you dig more or should I do it for you?" He said.

She panicked and told that he went to the mental asylum at the age of 7 as he was extremely depressed..." She replied.

"Did he used to work in a morgue?" The officer investigated.

"Yes, but only for a few months..." She replied.

"Why was he expelled?" He asked.

Silence pertained.

"He used to brutally hit the dead bodies..." She cried.

She started crying even harder than before.

The shreds of evidence were submitted in front of the court which proved that the victim was not killed at the spot he was killed brutally afterward.

9

Split Together

by Rutika Pandya

9/09/2018
Pre-Confrontation

Nick, we have police inside our office, asking for you. What have you done?" My boss, Mr. Rihan Patel growled at me from the door of my cabin.

I had been careful while dealing with clients, even the ones whose names were pretty under the dirt in building business.

I don't know anything about it, he followed Mr. Patel to his cabin, where sub-inspector Ranjit Saha is waiting for me along with his team.

"Mr. Nick, I'm afraid we have to arrest you for culpable homicide amounting to murder." He said with finality.

A murder? A person dealing with papers and playing with money changing hands was accused of murder, "There is some mistake. How can I murder someone? I'm afraid of even bees." Hysteria might have found its way to my voice.

"Mr. Nick, we have eyewitnesses who saw you beat and bully one of your students, a 19-year-old, who is now dead. There is no mistake."

"Students? I work here, in this consultancy. I don't have students." I was numb. This was utter chaos.

"Tell me, Mr. Nick, does the right side of your abdomen hurt? Is there a healing bite mark on your neck?"

I had a weird pain in my abdomen, and something had been burning around my neck, I didn't know they were some kind of voodoo doctors who knew where it hurt. Nonetheless, what did all this have to do with the murder? I was in pain, how could I have murdered anyone?

I had been forcefully taken into custody, some kids and parents identified as their football coach; a farm owner on the outskirts who said he had leased a part of his land to me for teaching football to 19-20-year-old kids at a minimal price on weekends. How could I convince them that I hated football, and how much I liked sleeping in on weekends. They found dirty sports shoes, a football, and sports clothes in my apartment. They know I have a roommate to whom all this can belong to. However, they want to frame me and are bluffing that they have my fingerprints.

6/09/2018

The Worker

Looking at my name on the desk 'Nick' filled me with gratitude. With the current project under wraps, I could do with a higher salary and a bigger cabin. Can't wait to go home, order a nice dinner, and wake up late, because it's my last weekend as an executive. I will be the manager next weekend. Wish the clock ticks faster.

7/09/2018

The Passion

Damn, the fool didn't wake me up. "Abhi, you fool. I'm late for practice again." I shout from my bed.

God, never bless anyone with such useless roommates.

"Bro, you said you wanted to turn off your phone and relax the whole weekend." Another excuse from Abhi from our living room.

"What do you mean by relax? Idiot. I have been relaxin' for the whole week. You're gonna regret it when I become the best footballer."

He'll be damned when I achieve something.

I made a protein shake and ran downstairs to find an autorickshaw and reach the outskirts of Ahmedabad to coach the dumb kids. So much to just stay in touch with football. Go make contacts, go make a name out of yourself they freaking say. I call bullshit. But I get to play football, that's what keeps me alive, literally, 'because that's what brings me food.'

Pretty late, and many of the parents have left, but the ones staying back are gonna beat the crap out of my head for being late, keeping their precious little kids waiting. Like I care.

"Hey kids, I told you to warm up by running along the field four times before I reach. Come on, come on, we will all do it together. One-two, one-two, come on." I shout as I run towards the field to avoid nagging.

As we complete the rounds, I start with a basic one on one practice. One kid stands in front of the net, one does the goalkeeping. Twenty-five kids, twelve pairs of two, and one dumb kid who doesn't know where to look and thinks of himself as Jan Oblak. That freak just knows how to jump within the net. I am gonna perfect him today. He will start and end the practice, just goalkeeping.

"Come on, you Oblak, focus. It has been an hour. Don't dive. Last 10 kicks. I want perfection." I shout as I try to keep my anger in wraps.

For five balls he manages to give goals, on the sixth, it comes straight to his face, and the stupid kid just stands there like a stupefied deer. God have mercy on this kid when I go at him.

I lose my cool and charge at him, slap him awake into this world; stand in front of him, and kick the ball, straight onto his chest. The guy doesn't dunk. I repeat the same 10 times. The sensitive human says something is broken in his chest; I say it's his fragile ego. I hate dumbness. I drag him up while he spits on me, mouths a bad word, and puts up a finger. I lost it again. We start fighting, twenty-five 19-20-year-old kids, and a 35-year-old coach. I was hurt, I felt a sharp pain behind my neck, but I slammed Oblak into the pole and ran. I don't care if he is hospitalized. I'm never coming back here. It's over. I will be getting a job in Arya Public school as a coach next Monday. My life is set. My first goal is scored.

I take an autorickshaw and go back home. Those kids managed to even hit me in the abdomen. Damn those kids.

I reach home, head straight into the bathroom, and swear not to wake up early tomorrow. To hell with those kids, I will coach in the school and earn a name for myself by winning tournaments.

My roommate came to help me when he saw me stumbling. He tells me that my neck is bleeding, I would have to clean myself first.

08/09/2018

"Dude, wake up. I have brought you an ointment for your injury from yesterday. And, bro, you need to tell me what happened. I can't go on not knowing where you were the whole week, and especially the weekends." Yells my roommate from the kitchen as he cooks eggs for us.

"I told you I just wanted to enjoy my weekend in my bed. Where the hell would I go? You know I'm a shy person. I stay in my room all weekend." I reply, my voice is still groggy from sleep. I slept so well that my body is aching from sleeping in one position.

"Mr. Nick, are you high on drugs?" Abhi jokes, but I hear a genuine doubt in his voice.

"Well, sometimes I forget what I had been doing, like blackout memories. I could use some drugs for that. Until then, sober is good. Once I get a raise, I'm gonna go see a shrink." I'm awake now, and I head to the bathroom.

10/10/2018

The Torture

It has been 24-hours since they have been questioning me. They say they have found every piece of evidence against me, along with eyewitnesses. They even had two autorickshaw drivers identify me in sports gear. My roommate and my boss have testified against my suspicious and mysterious behaviour. I can't have a lawyer of my choice. They have beaten me in anger. Parents of the kid whom I murdered tried to scratch my face. I can't even remember getting out of bed on the 7th. Was this a ploy by one of my clients? I have sweet-talked many investors into faulty projects, bribed many government officials on behalf of our consultancy, and used a fake name to get information. But everything was because I was supposed to do all that. The murder was a grave accusation. I would die before killing anyone, let alone a kid. How can I teach football? I had been the weakest footballer, I had been a depressed kid, I had been a silent adult all these years. But one day I'm accused of murder?

Police are generous in taking out all their frustration on my body. Of course, they should, if I was a murderer. But I'm not. The torture is breaking my soul, the guilt is crushing my soul. My bloody head cannot remember where the hell I was on the 7th. Abhi says I wasn't home the whole day, and came back at night, bleeding. I have read books about the whole world turning against a person, and they fight back. I'm alone, and I can't fight. I don't know whom to fight. There are too many blank spaces in my mind now.

30/11/2019

The Confrontation

It has been more than a year. I have been mauled in jail. I fought life until now. I fought with shitty food, vile stares, scattered beatings by the police, and death threats by my inmates. I have fought with the guilt of murdering someone. But I think today I'm going to embrace life and let go of the fight. I will allow life to take me into the world that rotates around souls. I feel the blood of that kid in my hands, I can taste it in my throat. I feel my hands tightening around his throat, I feel the rage, and yet it's not mine. I feel someone overpowering my mind and forcing me to do it. I feel trapped, screaming, screeching to not kill the kid. I see the light go out of his eyes. I panic, and I wake up. The last-minute nightmare is draining the life out of me, I think this nightmare is going to kill me finally. I need to rest, forever.

NICK is gone today. He died in his sleep. But in reality, he died because he met his other-self. He had been a fragile kid, bullied because he liked football and couldn't play well. His parents had left him to stay with his grandparents, who died within a week of each other's death, while Nick was a teenager. Just before their death, Nick had an episode of severe bullying in school, physical as well as mental. He was kicked and thrashed by the school football team. Teachers called him 'girly' to cry at such a silly thing (Feminism still has a long way to go.) Everyone had to outcast him because, during the episode of bullying, he had peed his pants. A real dishonour if you're a teenager. He secluded himself completely after his grandparents' death. But his brain decided to give him relief by birthing an aggressive personality that never stood against bullshit, that would be confident and passionate for football but remain hidden beneath his fragile, sensitive, and sane personality. It hadn't been a problem for him, except for memory lapses, and sudden monachopsis; his brain was sly in managing both the personalities. All this, until one day he saw a kid just like him. Instead of understanding him, the aggression that he had built up all these years, drove his soul to violence. It killed the kid, and it killed himself too. He knew something was wrong, all along. He knew he had been trapped; he just didn't know-how. If he had gotten psychological help, if he had his parents by his side, if he wasn't bullied, two lives of his world would have been saved. 'If only' people understood that their actions might have consequences. 'If only' people gave preference to mental well-being.

Nick died when his split personalities came together to show him a mirror. Nick died knowing that he was no longer trapped, he was liberated.

10

The Tale Of Two Sisters

by Swikriti Lahoty

I pretend to sleep, tucked under my blanket when my brother walks into the room. He locked the room behind him, unzipping his pants. I tried to push him away but as always he came and he was all over me, removing his pants and pushing himself in me, grunting and groaning. I don't cry anymore. I just lay down quietly, not making a sound and imagining what it would feel like having my twin sister with me, the braver one of us who let me live and died to give me life before even coming into this world. I think about her, my mind going blank. I am brought back by the stinging pain in my cheeks when my brother slapped me.

"Tell that to me again and I will kill you!" He said.

I just was silent like always taking it all in. I have never been able to speak, the reason unknown. Sometimes I think it's fate. I killed my sister so I lost my voice, the voice that could have given me the freedom to fight against all this. When he is done, he zips his pants and saunters out of the room.

The next morning during breakfast, my brother gives me his evil smirk and I look down at the food. He finishes his breakfast and so does the father and they leave, leaving their plates for me to pick and scrub. Mother tells me to miss school today because my brother's friends are coming home for dinner. I feel the anger rising in me and maybe it is expressed on my face because my mother yells at me that if I ever react that way, counter her or disobey her, I will be thrown out of the house, to fend for myself.

"Freak!" She mutters under her breath.

That's what they all call me. My mother often tells me that I ate my sister before coming into this world, took her away from the world, and since then she has been a captive in my body, trying to outgrow me and become who she was destined to be and not someone like me, weak and a freak.

At night, I serve the three-course meal my mother has prepared for my brother's friends. They come over often, to eat and relax, to be doted on by my mother, and to make fun of me. They have always enjoyed that. My parents never objected and I had no voice, so the only thing I could do was to look angry and hiss at them and they would laugh at me saying my words didn't matter just like I didn't. Maybe if I had my sister, she would stand by my side, given words to the things I feel. I serve them quietly and they keep on making jokes. One of my brother's friends tells my mother how good she is to me for teaching me how life is going to be for me, that serving and working wordlessly was my destiny. My brother laughs heartily and tells them that he has been training me in his way for what my future would be. My hands shake from anger and red is all I see. I think of the words my sister would have said if she was alive, how she would have told me that I don't need their advice, least of all their concern for my future. When I open my eyes, I see all of them staring at me, some with irritation and my brother and father with outright anger. I quietly go to the kitchen and wash my face to calm my face down.

After dinner, my brother tells mom that he is going off with his friends to drop them and he will be late. He is going to smoke in that alley, I know already but my parents don't know or act as if they don't. While moving out he tells me that he has a birthday present for me for tomorrow and he will give it to me once he is back. That reminder of my birthday washes me with another wave of guilt and longing for my sister and I pray that maybe this birthday she would outgrow me, take over my body, and relieves me of all the pain that the world has inflicted on me.

I wash dishes when my mother cleans up everything and tells me to go down and buy some curd for tomorrow for my brother's favourite biryani. I grip the knife tightly in my hands, the edges cutting in my skin, coating it with my blood. I feel a rise of anger, the one unlike I have ever felt and I feel something shift inside me. Maybe, just maybe today my sister will come out and let me rest.

Done with all the chores, I go to sleep in my room half afraid that my brother would walk in after an hour or so and give me his 'GIFT!'

It was midnight.

I see a silhouette of the girl that looks eerily like me walking towards a smoker leaning on the wall of the alley smoking brazenly. She stealthily moves behind him and pushes the knife under his throat and whispers, "This is for my sister" and slices his throat. He falls on the floor, his own blood choking him, his eyes widened in shock. The girl beats him and looks up at me for the first time I see me with the kind of determination I never had.

I wake up with a gasp and find my mother shaking me.

At 4 in the morning, I was shaken. I woke up, frantic asking me if my brother met me or told me something about where he would be. I shake my head to say no. She keeps on crying saying that my brother never returned home last night. I look down and notice that these aren't the clothes I wore when I went to sleep. I ignore the thought of thinking of it as another weird thing about me. I try calming my mother down. My mother goes to the kitchen and I follow her. She fiddles with things to calm herself and I quietly observe her. She notices the knife freshly washed on the slab of the kitchen and yells at me for not keeping it in place. I just shrug trying to tell her I might have forgotten but she keeps on yelling. After a few minutes, my father and his friends come back home, face tired and drained out, and tear streaks covering their faces.

My father tells me that my brother was found by the police down the alley with his throat slit and face bruised and misshapen as if he was kicked on the face multiple times breaking his jaw and nose.

Maybe my sister has finally saved me the way I thought she would. After all, she lives inside me, and maybe from now on, we can share this body and this life.

11

Offense

by Dipali Talwar

In a world where you find everyone just running, competing, trying to achieve more than others; Vrinda was what-you-call-a-lively-girl. Her aspirations with her life were to lead a life of content and happiness, not bothering about any sought of competition. She was living in that bubble but then; life happened.

"Vrinda, when are you going to take anything seriously? Everything is a joke to you right?" Vrinda's mother was scolding her for not informing her about being late.

"Mumma, I am not a seven-year-old now. Just relax a bit. I'll inform you next time." She tried to evade the situation.

"I don't know when you will understand just one little thing that I don't object to you staying late outside but it won't kill you, to at least inform me that where you are supposed to be. I get so worried about you."

"I understand! Now please just stop worrying this much." The mother-daughter duo calmed down after a while.

Vrinda's mother, Meera was a strong independent lady, raising her daughter alone. Though a composed person, Meera would always lose it when it came to Vrinda's safety. She wanted all that was best for Vrinda. She got pregnant with Vrinda, out of wedlock and you know the societal pressure, but she didn't bow down to it. She decided to raise her unborn child alone, putting on a strong face, but deep down, she was always scared. Even the tiniest thing could frighten her. Despite the daily routine of debates over safety, Vrinda remained the same spontaneous person and Meera, the same worrying mother.

The next morning.

Vrinda got ready for the office. With a chapati roll in her mouth, she told her mother, "I might be late today, this meeting is really important and might take more time to finalize than expected." She left in a hurry.

"All the best. And be careful!" Meera shouted while Vrinda crossed the threshold of the door.

Vrinda was on her way to the office, taking the same route as usual but today the traffic was relatively low. Finding the roads almost clear, she rushed towards the office. She was riding her scooty at the speed of 60 km per hour. For a two-wheeler, it's quite a speed. She saw a man trying to pass her from the rear-view mirror. She felt a bit strange that with all that space, he was still not overtaking her, so she decelerated a bit and gave him more space to cross.

As soon as she slowed down, that man brought his vehicle parallel to her and grabbed her breast. She didn't know what just happened. She screamed. As she reacted, the man tried to run. He sped away leaving Vrinda was in a pool of emotions. She didn't want to just be a victim, so she tried to chase that man for a while. She kept shouting cuss words and followed him till he took a sharp turn and disappeared into one of the streets. Vrinda didn't know what she was supposed to do now. So, she just kept driving towards her office.

She kept thinking about the incident but she had turned into a cold statue. She parked the scooty in the parking area when two of her colleagues, Meghna and Shivika arrived. They were in a good mood and asked Vrinda humorously if she was following them. She didn't respond. They asked her to come fast as they were already late. They turned to see Vrinda still standing at the same spot. They came to her. Vrinda finally spoke.

"Some bastard just grabbed my breast on the way, guys."

The words left Vrinda's mouth to shock Meghna and Shivika. Their eyes widened in shock to hear this. Vrinda narrated the whole incident to them. Shivika instantly hugged Vrinda tightly to give her some sense of security. Meghna was holding her hand. They suggested that Vrinda should go back to her house, rather they offered to take her back. They told her to get some rest and take a day off. "I am not going to sit at home just because some jerk doesn't know boundaries," Vrinda said.

"We understand, we just want you to know that we are there for you okay. You should file a complaint against him."

"Oh, I sure do want to get that bastard arrested but I don't know him, even if I want to, I couldn't recognize him. It's kind of all blurry right now. I remember, he turned to see that I was chasing him, but I don't remember his face."

"Did you get his license plate number?"

"No!"

The girls found themselves at the crossroads where they didn't know how to react. There was sympathy, anger, shock, and what not in the air. They went into the office when Vrinda assured them that she was fine and can handle this day.

She was wrong.

While giving the presentation at the meeting, she broke down. She couldn't breathe. She felt like throwing up. Meghna took her away while Shivika handled the rest of the meeting. Despite not being able to stand, Vrinda was obstinate to manage this day. She didn't want to just go home. She wiped her tears, drank some water, and sat in her cubicle in front of her laptop. She survived the day.

Before leaving for home at the end of the day, Meghna and Shivika asked to accompany her back home, the offer which was immediately denied. She wanted to face the world alone. She knew if she hid behind the protection of her friends right now, she would not be able to go on that particular road alone ever again. She wanted her confidence back.

She was full of rage. She reached home and ate dinner, had a good conversation with Meera without a single mention of the day's incident. Many times, she felt she would just cry in her mother's lap but she stopped herself every time. Her mother was her best friend. She would tell every single detail of her life to her. Meera was like a sanctuary to her, but when she wanted to talk about the most horrifying experience of her life, she found herself without any words.

She excused herself to her room. As soon as she shut the door close, she felt wobbly. She sat on the floor and cried her heart out. She knew it was not her fault in any way that she should feel bad about but it felt as if her soul was wounded. She felt wronged. She felt dirty. She stood under the shower, trying to "clean" herself.

The next day she woke up with teary eyes. She didn't realize she was crying the whole night. She got ready for a new day. She was second doubting taking the same route today but she was sure of one thing, she had to go and go on the same route. She was filled with a fire that wanted to burn that man if he came again.

After this incident, she could not keep herself in the right mind. She became obsessed with winning. She saw every male colleague as a competitor. She immersed herself into her work and a race to outrun everybody in the office. A carefree Vrinda turned into a cutthroat, driven person. She got promoted because of all the extra work she had been doing to keep herself busy.

Working the whole day, nights were an especially difficult time for Vrinda. She would often cry to sleep. She started seeing her alter ego who would console her and talk to her. It was as if she was filling a void of her mother's presence with her alter ego.

Once, even Meghna caught Vrinda talking to herself through a mirror in the office restroom. She got worried and offered to go see a therapist with Vrinda. To which, Vrinda abruptly denied saying she was just giving herself a pep talk for a meeting.

It had been months; the man didn't come back after her. She kept on taking the same route despite her friends telling her to change the route. Whenever any vehicle would come near her trying to take a pass, Vrinda's heart would race so fast that its beating could be heard from a mile away. Mere horn would keep her on her toes. She would always remind herself that if this type of thing ever happens again, she would just beat the hell out of that person.

One year later.

Vrinda was dreading today for about a week now. Today it would be a whole year since the traumatic incident. She was all worked up. She went to work and the day went well. She was proud of herself for surviving the whole day. She felt that time had maybe healed her a bit.

Some days later when she was coming back from the office, a person started to catcall her in the middle of the road. He passed some illicit comments on her dress and her body. He was not letting her pass. Shockingly, Vrinda didn't say a word to him. She didn't even feel the emotion in her body as if she just blocked the whole scene from her mind.

When she came back home, a sudden rush of emotions attacked her. She realized what had happened. Alter Vrinda kept shouting at her, for being such a coward. She felt angrier and angrier on herself for not saying anything, not standing up for herself. She threw her phone at her shouting alter-self. When that man grabbed her, though she could not catch him, she still stood up for her, she had a voice. But now; she felt strange.

"Why didn't I say anything?" She wondered.

She was in that turmoil when Meera found her sitting on the floor near the door. She helped Vrinda get up and asked what had happened. Vrinda didn't say a word. Meera hugged her and asked again. In her mother's embrace, Vrinda felt like a child again, a safe child. She told her the whole story.

Vrinda cried her heart out in Meera's lap. When she could not answer why she could not say anything today to the creep, Meera came up with an answer. "You were so traumatized by the first incident, that the second; didn't seem such a big deal to you. You felt all this time that you had dealt with your turmoil but you were not there yet. You just needed to talk to me, love. When I was about your age, I experienced something similar and couldn't tell my mother anything because I knew even if I told her, it would be counted as my fault, just like my pregnancy. But you, my dear, can share anything with me."

Talking to Vrinda, Meera realized that she had to stop being scared herself to protect her daughter. She felt empowered talking about her own experience after this whole time.

It all made sense to Vrinda now. She had been jumpy this whole year but just talking to Meera gave her peace of mind. She felt at home again.

"Vrinda, an offence is an offence, be it of any scale. What happened with you a year ago, was wrong. But you can't measure it on a measuring scale. What happened today was also wrong. You should have given that man your piece of mind at that very moment. And darling, don't ever wait for someone to come to your rescue, you have to do that for yourself. You are strong.", Meera said holding Vrinda in her arms.

Talking to Meera gave Vrinda clarity on her whole situation. She promised herself that she won't just be a victim of the toxic behaviour of anyone. But again, she kind of promised that a year ago as well. What do you think, would she be able to keep her promise to herself this time or fall prey to her insecurities yet again? Will alter-Vrinda return?

12

The Unsent Letters

by Muskan Kamwani

At times we always see the brighter side of that happy-go-lucky kind of girl like Della. She always brought smiles wherever she went, it always seemed like she turned everything into gold. The way her smile glittered the room was remarkable. She could never leave a sliver in your life where you can just sink into the dark corners. Is it even necessary for you to be sad around Della? But still, I am hanging in my darkness and I am okay with it. I still love gazing at you Della, it consumes me and pulls me off, from those darker ends of my life. The ends where I can't stop myself to kill another life of a monster like Jason. I know he lives down the road, he is a teenager, moreover, I don't even know him. Still, I had an urge to kill him... I know I don't have the right to take things into my hand as a citizen. Yet, I killed him, Della... I killed one more monster last night... And I felt good I know I should not have done that but I did it anyway... It felt like he should be burned alive and trust me I poured acid over him... I heard his screams... Him in the pain which I think he should surely go through... And not even for a single second I felt pity for that moron. So I killed him... I know you will hate me for this love but he deserved it. I know I can never confront myself or even reveal my identity to you, Della. But no matter how amazing I feel in the darkness deeply rooted inside me. I will never stop loving you. I will always love you. I will go to any extent to just make you feel okay and convinced about the reason I gave you in my first letter. I can never stop sending you these letters until you realize why I murdered all those monsters from Josh, Jackson, Jim, Jonathan, Jenson, Justin, Jacob, John, Jared, Joshua, and the one I killed last night Jason. I should not have done that, but I think they should go through the same pain I just wrote about. And the same pain I forced them to go through. I laughed at their face, the way I did when I killed the first one. I don't want to forgive them and I never will, Della. I buried their burnt corpses at the same place. I know you won't like it at all, but I love you, Della. I will always protect you and never let anyone hurt you. 'M' and I will always love you and be your shields. Again, we won't be found, Della. We are long gone and hiding under these notices, news of these missing people. I will soon tell you our names.

Lots Of Love

H"

It was the 11ᵗʰ letter Della got, she still had no guts to gather herself and tell her little sister Roma what she was going through. How scary these letters are for her. Della was emotionless at that moment again. Her smile that brought glory to a sad corner was missing somewhere. Roma was so busy with her work that whenever she saw that sorrow in her sister she had no time to go and discuss it out with her. She knew no matter how happy she makes everyone she still is an introvert. She sticks to her diaries and imaginations to work on the stories she wants to write. Roma was oblivious about the heavy heart Della was carrying on for a month now. Every time Della wanted to talk to Roma about these murders and missing people, she was silent. Every time Roma's forehead had lines of anger, Della never tried to start the conversation about what she read from those murderers about whom the police officers and news reporters are looking for. She never wanted to confront those murderers, she wants to stop everything for a second and take a deep breath to calm herself from all those horrible things she read about the murders of those missing people.

The 12th Letter

"My name is 'Hannah' and the other one's name is 'Millie' and we are your shields. Not only yours but Roma's too. I know yours and Roma's parents divorced when you were 8 years and Roma was 4 years. Your mother became involved with a man named Johnny who was abused with drugs, primarily hemp seed or cannabis. And he started to abuse you sexually. I have heard the cries of your heart Della when you were just 12. He kisses your mother, but how can you guys tell her that he kissed you too. That moron broke all his limits when once he got high and forced you to give him a blow job, poor little Roma was not able to help you out. That little girl didn't even know what just he did to you and forced you to do.

Not only this, once, when you were 16, he brought you redwings, that time too he just wanted to quench his thirst for lechery. He indulged in the ocean of lust, rays of lies; it was just his mere fantasy for your mother and not love your mother expected and always yearned for. And these dreadful incidents tore her!

Broke you down into pieces,

like useless bits of paper.

As long as you relieved this loathing incident on a loop in your mind, I know it scared the shit out of you and you were numb. You felt defenseless. However soon you realized, you are not defenseless.

You are powerful and no matter how much the garden behind that old factory tormented you, you still had the strength to protect yourself and Roma. You are the strongest girl, we have ever met. And we are the shields for you and Roma. That's the place where all those 11 rapists and eve-teasers deserved to die and be buried. We did the right thing for you and Roma.

Lots Of Love

Hannah And Millie"

Della read this letter and was trembling out of fear, she cried her heart out and ran out of the house and shouted that she is going out to have an ice-cream. But Roma ignored every deadline she had about her work and halted Della's room. She saw the half-opened old black laced but a torn box, which she knew what it had... She got the courage to see it and she saw Hannah and Millie, their dolls. They wrote 'H' and 'M' specifically on those dolls. She had a flashback of what Della went through holding those dolls, whispering, and crying for help. Because their dad gave it to them long ago.

And he always said *"At times the dolls protect you from all the sorrows you go through and protect you just like an angel does. Never let these dolls die, always keep them alive."*

Suddenly Roma saw some letters. She opened them and read those letters and she was mortified. She saw Della's handwriting. Roma had no words to put forward and make a legitimate statement. She didn't understand what made Della write those letters. But they made some sense.

Maybe some secrets are better buried alive, just the way Della's characters were caged in the void. The void that had a shape, a figure, a reason, and a body but never had a voice of its own. Roma stood still and started crying how she was unaware that those letters were written by Della and still, she kept *'Hannah'* and *'Millie'* alive.

13

The Rehab

by Shaymi Shah

Ved Archarya was an orphan who belonged to the suburban area of Mumbai. He was about twelve years old when his guardian, Manish Agrawal, adopted him and brought him to Mumbai. At a very early age, he had decided he wanted to pursue acting as a career.

He was always looking for opportunities to develop his acting skills. Whether it was taking part in the plays happening with his theatre group in college or playing smaller roles in some advertisements, he would take it up with utmost enthusiasm. Most of his teenage and schooling years went by studying hard in the day and working on his acting skills at night.

He had struggled a lot to make his way through the entertainment industry. Finally, he got assigned the role of a supporting actor in a big film project for which he even won the best debut award that year. That was his breakthrough project. After this, his career took a whole new turn. Soon he started getting more offers for movies. In the meanwhile, he had fallen deeply in love with Simran Ahuja, one of the co-actors for a film. They got married within the next few months.

It was as if everything in his life was moving in fast forward. His career was reaching its peak, he was married to the love of his life and they even had a beautiful daughter who was now five years old. And then, one night, while coming home from a dinner party, they met with an accident.

He survived but his wife and daughter died on the spot. He suffered from trauma for months. He tried engaging in activities that would help him move on. He eventually sought medical help, took sleeping pills, but nothing seemed to help him. He started drinking, smoking, and taking drugs, hoping that it would help him get rid of this feeling of emptiness. He finally spoke to his guardian to take him to a rehab center. They figured it was probably the best way for him to get better.

His therapist had been given an overview of his condition- he was suffering from PTSD- Post-Traumatic Stress Disorder.

His day began at six in the morning, followed by yoga, meditation classes, and a healthy breakfast. He would get time to freshen up and take a shower before attending the group therapy session at 11 o'clock. Then after lunch, he would speak to his therapist in a one-on-one session about his feelings and get recommendations on what he could do to feel better. He would get time to relax and do something he liked to do during the evenings before dinner. That was the time when he would take a swim or sometimes play a game of chess with a fellow patient.

By 6 pm, he would again attend a short group therapy session, after which he would go for his daily walk in the garden, have an early dinner, and then go to his room.

He would meet a few of his closest friends after dinner. It was his most favorite time of the day. It was a secret that they had kept from the people working at the rehab center. The patients weren't usually allowed to see each other after dinner. They were supposed to take time to be alone and contemplate everything they had learned during the day.

But Kunj, Deep and Parin were the ones who gave him company in times when he felt lonely and sad. They knew what he was going through and wanted to help him to get better. They would often make plans of even escaping from Rehab, but none of them dared to take action.

Kunj was a national-level swimmer. He had won gold medals in several swimming competitions. He was proud, but he was sad that he had no one to share it with except his friends. He had no close family to take care of him. He had realized at a very early age that he could rely only upon himself.

Once during his pre-swimming training sessions, his shoulder got injured and dislocated. He had even tried months of physiotherapy but, he was told that though he might be able to do light exercises, he wouldn't be able to swim anymore. He couldn't believe that it was going to be the end of his career in swimming. He hadn't ever thought about what he would do if he couldn't swim.

He started getting panic attacks and nightmares about drowning because his hands wouldn't move. His condition started deteriorating very quickly, and he thought it was best to get treated and be fit mentally. Only then he would be able to work on improving his performance physically. That's how he had ended up in Rehab. It was his voluntary decision.

Deep, on the other hand, had a very different story. He was an employee at a corporate company. He had worked for over three years, rigorously for the company. He would always be present at the office on time. He would even stay late if his boss needed him to finish some work last moment. He knew his boss was very arrogant and demanding, but he kept working hard to make sure he remained in his good books. He was going to get promoted to a senior-level post this year. He was so excited and happy that all his hard work was going to pay off. But, somehow, at the last moment, his boss had changed his mind. He had given the promotion to one of his colleagues. At that moment, Deep lost his temper and attacked his boss. They had to call security to take him away from the office. A police complaint was filed against him.

After a few days of investigation, the police found out that he had been taking drugs to keep himself up at night to work. On the day of the attack, he had been sleep-deprived for three days and overdosed before coming to the office to keep himself alert. He was assigned to Rehab till he became mentally fit to work again.

He often wondered how different everything would be if he had just listened to his heart and pursued a career in theatre rather than doing this machine-like corporate job at an office. For him, going to rehab was involuntary but necessary.

Parin was the one who was going through depression for two years now. He was a writer who had tried to win the hearts of people through his deeply thoughtful stories and quotes. His dream was to become a best-selling author someday. He kept pitching his manuscripts to different publishing houses, but none of them took his work seriously. They would promise him that they would read his manuscript, but they never did. Upon confrontation, a few of them gave excuses saying they would get back to him, but he never got any calls.

Over a period of time, he started realizing that he was getting played. He decided to take up a loan from a bank and self-publish his book. He started working, day and night, editing, and finalizing the manuscript before it went into printing.

After months of intensive hard work, he finally published the book. He waited for a few weeks to check the response, but he realized it was a disaster. His dream was far from becoming a reality and he was broke as he had put all his savings into his book. He couldn't bear the losses he had incurred. He had even attempted to commit suicide.

Fortunately, his housemaid saw him before he could jump off the balcony and pulled him back. She told his neighbour (and his close friend) about it right away. He took him to a psychiatrist the next day who said he was diagnosed with Major depression and he would need to be put in Rehab right away. That was the only place that would make sure that he didn't attempt to take his life again.

Parin made sure he still wrote every day. It was something that made him feel calm and relaxed during the day. But it was also the same thing that reminded him of his failed book every night. Every morning he would be full of hope and positivity, and every night, the dark thoughts would take over his mind and make him feel weak again.

Ved was listening to his friends, telling him their stories. They were the ones that made him feel understood. They made him feel safe. Suddenly, they all heard a voice. They became quiet.

From the dark corner of the room, Abhay appeared in front of them. A devilish smile spread across his face, rage in his eyes. From the expression on his face, one could guess that something very evil was going on in his mind.

Ved and his friends were wondering why they hadn't realized that someone had entered the room. He moved towards them and commanded them to pay attention at once.

He told them he had a plan. He was going to get them all out of here. He told them how he had heard that the nurses and the doctors were keeping them drugged so that they felt weak and never attempted to escape. He had found out that the place that they all thought was Rehab was actually Prison. They weren't patients. They were prisoners who had been punished for crimes they hadn't even committed.

The rest of them got very confused. They weren't able to comprehend what was going on. Was Abhay real or, were they all hypnotized? Was this hallucination a side effect of the medications they had been given earlier after dinner today?

They started panicking and asking questions all at the same time. Abhay tried to tell them that if they didn't lower their voice someone would find out about them. But they didn't listen. They got worried and started screaming, shouting abusive words out of anger.

Just at that moment, a nurse was passing by the room. She heard loud voices coming from the room. She quickly asked one of the caretakers to accompany her and slowly opened the door. She couldn't believe what she saw.

Ved was talking in a different tone and language every few seconds. It seemed like he hadn't noticed their presence in the room. He suddenly looked up at the nurse, the same devilish smile on his face and caught her off guard. The nurse screamed out of fear and the caretaker ran to call security. In the next moment, he was on top of her, trying to strangle her. The caretakers and four other guards came running towards the room and pulled Ved off of the nurse. She was barely able to breathe.

When his therapist came in, he saw the diary that was kept open on his bedside table, and the page was titled Ved. He closed the diary and was shocked to see that it belonged to Abhay. He quickly flipped its pages and saw stories about Ved, Kunj, Deep and, Parin in it. Even the handwriting of the stories was different as though, completely different people had written it. The therapist had misdiagnosed the condition of this patient.

Ved once again had proved to be a successful actor by giving the best performance of his life and made someone believe in people or things that didn't even exist. Abhay and the rest gave him a round of applause.

14

Annamarie

by Manoj Vaz

Raj couldn't believe his ears. Their engagement was fixed for January 18 and on New Year's Eve, Tanushri had called him to break up with him.

"It's not you, Raj..." She explained, "You are a sweet guy. I am not ready for a commitment."

"Then why would you say yes in the first place?" Raj had tears flowing down his cheeks.

"I just got a letter of acceptance from SHL in Switzerland. They have accepted my application for BSC in Hospitality Science with a partial scholarship." She tried to explain.

"But we can get engaged. I will happily wait for you for two years." He clutched at straws, hoping against hope.

"Raj, I can't spend two years in Switzerland in fetters." She sounded distant, "It's a new life that has started for me."

"How can you equate my love to fetters?" Raj couldn't believe his ears.

"That's the point, Raj. I love you but I am not in love with you. Sorry, dear. Like I said before, it's not you, it's me."

He wanted to say, "What about our families? What about me? The humiliation I will face?" And so many questions. But he had heard enough.

He shut himself from everybody at home.

Some of his relatives said, "We told you so! You should have hitched up with a nice Punjabi girl, but instead, you went for a Bengali! Haven't you heard the old British saying about what to do when you encounter a snake and a Bengali?"

Others, especially his mother, looked at him with pity, like he was a shivering wet puppy. The latter was worse.

He didn't have a lot of friends in Delhi. A software programmer at a multinational meant a lot of late hours. He had lost contact with all his school and college friends. Where was the time to meet people and make friends? Raj was hardly an extrovert. He met Tanu online and he fell madly in love with her in less than a month.

Being a software programmer also meant that he had no escape from work. When he was not in the office, he was working from home. There he was at home, immersed in work at 9:00 pm after an early dinner with the usual puppy dog sympathy and the "I told you so." Symphony when his phone beeped. It was a text message on his Instagram account.

"Hi, Raj. This is Marie from Cochin, Kerala. Can we be friends?"

Raj wasn't sure. He came across all sorts of weirdos on these social networking sites. Women soliciting. Men pretending to be women. Scamsters trying to entice you off your money. He was especially wary of 'women' making the first move. And going with his current diaspora in the luck department, he expected the worst.

But curiosity got the better of him and he probed her photo album and 'about' information. Marie George seemed like a shy, pretty, 20-year-old BArch student from Cochin.

Before he knew it, he was pouring his heart out to her. Marie had the patience of hearing him out without sounding condescending. Finally, around 3:00 am, he bid her good night and fell asleep with a smile on his lips.

The next day, on his way to work, he texted her. Every time, his phone beeped at work, his heart leaped a bit, but it was not Marie returning his text. With a frown, he returned to his mundane work.

Mr. Chopra, his boss, was more than his usual gregarious self that day.

"He probably must have got news of my disengaged engagement." He smiled at his wordplay, "Nothing gives more pleasure to bosses than the misery of their subordinates!"

That evening after dinner, Raj received Marie's text.

"I am usually very busy with my projects and assignments during the day." She explained, "I hope you understand."

"Sure, I was at work too." He replied, trying to sound casual.

Over the next few months, they chatted every day. Marie was his dream girl. She was sweet and understanding.

An Anglo-Indian born and brought up in Cochin, she was 5 feet 4, with long, dark curly hair, an oval face, and bluish-grey eyes, surely a gift from her British antecedent. Her father, Thomas, was a school principal and her mother, Gracie, ran a handicraft shop in the upmarket M.G. Road of Cochin.

As days went by, Raj began to smile again like people smile when they are in love. Marie seemed to have changed his luck at work too. Mr. Chopra was appreciating him more and the other programmers asked him for advice when they got stuck.

One thing was odd though. Marie never indulged in video chat though he wanted to do it so often.

She told him that she had sworn not to use a mobile phone till she completed her BArch and chatted only through her laptop which did not have a cam.

He laughed it off as an Anglo-Indian idiosyncrasy.

Then on Monday morning, Mr. Chopra called him to his cabin.

"Raj, I have good news. We have landed the ASES ERP implementation project we had pitched for last month. We will need our best programmer to go to Austin on a one-year contract and spearhead the implementation. I hope you have your passport ready!"

Accommodation and transport were taken care of, the pay (because it was in USD) was four times what he got in India. It was what every software programmer in India dreamt of.

His family was ecstatic.

His mother had a question though, "Was Texas in Canada? I can ask Raghuveer to pick you up from the airport." Half of his extended family from his maternal side were settled in Canada, mostly working as supermarket salesmen or Uber drivers. The afore-mentioned Raghuveer Chacha even owned a hotel in Ontario.

"No, Momma." He patiently replied, "Austin is the capital of the state of Texas in the United States of America."

It was on an impulse that he decided to visit Cochin and surprise Marie by personally giving her the good news.

Since he did not have her postal address, he tracked her mother's handicraft shop and from there tracked her phone number and residential address.

With a smile on his face, he booked his ticket to Cochin for the coming Sunday.

After the debacle with Tanu, he hadn't disclosed his relationship with Marie to his family. So, he said, he was traveling to Cochin for work. Anyway, he had booked the late-night flight back to Delhi.

He landed in Cochin at around 9:00 am and took an Uber to M. G. Road. To his surprise, the drive was over an hour. The new fully solar-powered, state-of-the-art international airport was indeed quite far from the city.

It was around noon when he knocked on the door of an independent house in the 4th Cross Lane of M. G. Road. The door was opened by a sweet-looking, middle-aged lady.

"Hi!" He said, "I am Raj Sharma from Delhi."

He was met with a blank stare.

"I am Marie's friend. I assume you are Gracie George, her mother."

"Y... Yes, I am." the lady replied as she was joined by a young man of Raj's age.

"Mommy, who's this?" The young man queried.

"H... He says he is Marie's friend." She stuttered.

The young man faced Raj, "Hi, I am Jacob. How long has it been since you connected with her?"

"I chatted with her last night," Raj was getting a little confused at all the fuss.

"Why don't you come in?" The man said, "Mommy, can you make a cup of tea for Raj. He looks tired and weary after a long journey."

"Yes... Yes..." replied Gracie and disappeared into the kitchen while Jacob led Raj to a comfortable sofa in the living room.

As he entered Raj saw two garlanded photo frames on the wall. One was of a middle-aged man and the other was of his Marie.

Raj collapsed onto the sofa! He was speechless.

Gracie brought him a glass of water which he gulped down to gain a bit of composure.

"Is... Is that Marie?" He stuttered.

"Yes. Marie and my husband, Thomas, died in an accident last year." Gracie said as she placed the cup of tea on the table.

"B... But how can that be? I have been chatting with her every day for the last 2 months!"

"That can be explained," Jacob said.

"You see, Marie has a twin, Anna, who was in the car when the accident took place. Whereas Marie and my dad succumbed on the spot, Anna was grievously injured and in a coma for 15 days." He continued, "When she came out of a coma, she was diagnosed with Dissociative Identity Disorder or DID."

"DID?" Raj had no idea what it meant.

"Dissociative Identity Disorder is a rare condition in which two or more identities, or personality states, take control of an individual. Some people describe this as an experience of possession. The person also experiences extensive memory loss." Jacob explained.

"How does that explain my conversations with Marie?" Raj was still perplexed.

"Come with me." Jacob beckoned.

He took Raj by his arm to a room that was locked from outside. He opened it softly and both entered.

Inside was Marie. With dishevelled locks and bloodshot greyish blue eyes. She was wearing a nightgown and her left foot was chained to the iron bedpost. She growled when she saw them.

"This is Anna." Introduced Jacob, "We have to keep her in chains because she can get quite violent during the day. But usually, in the night, she is quite serene."

"We always chatted at night," Raj said.

"She has a laptop with Wi-Fi which she uses. It's one of the small privileges that she has. We don't want to take that away from her." Jacob overcame those emotions.

"She has frequent memory lapses. Especially in the daytime. In case you want to continue chatting with her, she won't remember that you were here." Jacob looked downcast.

"Yes, I will continue chatting with Marie." Raj replied with a resolution, "She had been good to me. She gave me the strength to pick myself up after I was broken. She brought sunshine and luck to my life. I am forever indebted to her!"

That night when he was flying back to Delhi. He couldn't stop thinking about Marie or was she, Anna? Or Annamarie? Whoever she was, she was his guardian angel and he would not let go of her.

It was early morning when the plane landed in Delhi, he switched on his phone and he had a missed call. It was from Tanu.

He knew he would wake her up but he called her from the Uber, anyway. She answered sleepily.

"Hi Raj," She said, "I am back in Delhi. The agent who got me admission to SHL was a scamster. Dad and I went all the way to Lucerne in Switzerland only to learn that all the documents were forged and the agent made off with the 2000 Euro that we paid as advance."

"Oh, that's terrible." Raj reacted, genuinely sorry for her.

"I was wondering if we could meet up and start where we left off." Tanu continued.

"Oh, Tanu!" Raj replied, "I wish we could. But my office is sending me out to Austin, Texas, next month for a year on a contract."

"So what?" Tanu replied, "We can get engaged and I will wait for a year for you to return."

"Tanu, I can't spend a year in Texas in fetters." He replied, "It's a new life that has started for me."

He knew he had to thank Annamarie for giving him the strength to say what he did.

15

Tale Of An Aching Heart

by Honey Patel

Moksh

Doctor, there is an emergency case, we will have to get intubation done."

"Shift the patient from ER to ICU. Prepare for intubation. Quick." Moksh replied.

Moksh was posted in for night duties in an emergency ward.

He dreamt of becoming a surgeon and there he was! Working in a corporate hospital paying him a hefty amount for his dream career.

Alas! We end up hating things we desired as kids. Worse when a feeling of regret takes over that you chose to chase those desires that were... Baseless. Moksh never knew if he loved what he was doing for a living. Certainly, he wasn't happy but he could not even begin to think about leaving the surgery. Amidst existential crisis, there he was, trying to find himself a flicker of joy in evening runs and playing piano for himself.

Apart from being a doctor, Moksh played the Piano and sang songs to himself. This was a little secret that Moksh kept from the world. No one knew that he wrote and sang songs. Neither did Moksh mention anything about the talent he possessed.

"Moksh, we cannot give you leaves right now! We are seeing numerous cases of trauma this month." Dr. Vashishth snapped. "Another doctor is on her leaves as well."

"But Vashishth, knowing that I have been planning to take a few days off since the last few months, how could you grant leave to another doctor at the same time?"

Moksh somehow managed to convince their senior to allow him some days off.

Moksh left for the Fiji Islands the next day. There was a lot of turmoil to take his eyes off from. There were a lot of things he was feeling at once and he needed to take this burden off for a while. But he didn't know what awaits him at these beautiful islands.

On arrival, Moksh had already started feeling different. He felt as if a load of carrying an identity had been taken off his shoulders. He could be whatever that he wanted to be, do whatever he feels like doing during this trip, as no one knew him here.

Ruhi

Ruhi was trying to plan a trip with her friends for a long time but with a new job and pressure to establish a reputation, she did not want to start taking breaks from work within just two months of joining. She was putting in hard work to build an image in front of her seniors and she pulled it off well. It took her less time than she imagined to form friendly relations with her co-workers. She even put in extra hours at her work as she knew it was going to help her to ask for a week off.

Vacation

Ruhi and her friends would go to random bars at night for drinks and dinner during their vacation. One evening, they went to a place which was a bit dark and noisy. The bar vibed well with them and everyone got carried away with music. For some reason, Ruhi was a bit distracted and glanced outside the pub area now and then. A guy wearing a brown jacket was playing guitar on the poolside. He managed to gather a crowd humming to his song and enjoying his mesmerizing musical voice. Ruhi couldn't help but walk towards the pool across the bar. She was so enchanted by his music that she almost forgot to inform her friends about her whereabouts. She stood there, mesmerized by the song as if his music was a link connecting her world to his. She stood there, at a distance where she could listen to him clearly but couldn't make out who was playing it. There she was, listening to him, without blinking even once, as if her heart froze the moment to a standstill. Only if she could look at the face playing this beautiful tune!

Mayank

"Let us go to the same place from last night. Something about it was very beautiful." Ruhi told her friends convincingly.

Everyone gave in as all of them found the place very zen. Intending to see his face once, Ruhi went there along with her friends. He was there playing keyboard. The crowd that night was thicker. By the time Ruhi went there, it was harder to see the face of the keyboard player. She peeked at him once from afar but couldn't see him. Nevertheless, she was returning with songs to remember for a lifetime. Ruhi felt disappointed.

Everyone was sitting in the dining area and chitchatting when Ruhi excused herself for the restroom. There was a common narrow passage that was leading to both men's and women's restrooms. Since the restroom was occupied, Ruhi was waiting in the common lobby which was warmly lit and decorated with succulents and indoor plants. Although Ruhi did not want to, she ended up eavesdropping on two men's conversation. Their voices were clear enough to reach the common resting area and the door to the men's restroom was half-open.

"Being a musician, I keep traveling to different places. Besides, I never have to try to fetch offers or contracts, thankfully they just flow in."

"It must be cool being at different places and playing for different people... Sharing your story with them through your music. It must be a nice feeling to connect with so many people at once..."

"There is no story. I just happen to create them in my mind, weave words, and write songs. I feel that there are layers to myself, I just need to lift them turn by turn, layer by layer. I feel there are two very different worlds where I find myself torn in between constantly. There is this dull, weary feeling that tells me to stop stepping into both worlds. And I feel exhausted sometimes with this feeling. I do not know where it comes from. I do not know what worlds it is telling me to step out of. But I don't feel at home with it. Maybe that's where the music comes from. Sweet and sad, melancholic and forgiving, uncomfortable and homely. All I know is that it is not "cool" to be a part of it."

"That is a lot to take, Mayank!"

"You sound like an old man who has seen the world in its truest form."

"Somedays, I wake up with a feeling that I was living the life of some other person in my sleep. It keeps getting stranger. On waking up, I feel like I have been in someone else's mind, dreaming someone else's dreams and living in someone else's body. Some days, it is hard to believe that I have woken up in my own body."

After a moment, Mayank realized he had been talking all this while.

"As if, the things I told you before weren't strange enough. I almost scared you here." Mayank laughed.

All this while, Ruhi was overhearing their conversation. By now, she knew the guy Mayank was none other than the musician she wanted to see. As Ruhi went in, two men came out from the next door to leave the resting area.

India

"There you are!" Vashishth exclaimed almost excitedly on seeing Moksh.

"How was your trip?"

"It was nice. A bit jet-lagged though. But you know what, Vashishth... I would say the highlight of the trip was that I have never felt closer to home in a place so strange."

Moksh replied with gleaming eyes.

Moksh left for home in the evening.

'Moksh forgot this file on his desk again. He has to operate on this patient tomorrow. How could he forget to study the case!' Vashishth said to himself?

"Would you mind sending one of the interns to Moksh's house? This file needs to be sent today itself." He asked the hospital office staff.

Moksh's house

Moksh was sitting by the side of his piano with a cup of tea on a corner table when the intern arrived.

She listened aptly to the music Moksh was playing. It was not that Ruhi could not drop the file and leave. Something about Moksh made her dumbfounded. She felt more at home with the melancholic tune and she did not want to leave that moment.

Moksh was surprised to see an intern at his house. He welcomed her hesitantly. She gave him a warm smile. As soon as she handed over the file, she left without speaking a word.

That night, Ruhi left Mayank's house astonished.

Ruhi was utterly shocked. She couldn't stop thinking about how Moksh is the real name of Mayank. She kept rewinding Moksh playing piano and how happy and lost he seemed in his own little fabricated musical world. Moksh did not even notice Ruhi standing there when he was singing. He was not even closer to Dr. Moksh that Ruhi knew for the last few months. It was as if Dr. Moksh did not even exist. She started connecting dots in her mind. Ruhi realized that Mayank's character is so deep-rooted in Moksh's mind that he doesn't even know that he is torn between two personalities.

The next day, Ruhi went to Moksh's office to talk about his trip to the Fiji Islands.

"Sir, how do you manage trips to places afar just to sing?"

Moksh was befuddled. "What are you even talking about? Why would I go to different countries to sing? Also, when did I start singing? I just play the piano."

All her doubts were confirmed now. She knew that Moksh forced himself into burying his past that screamed music to an extent that his mind had started building a coping mechanism.

Bali (present-day)

Scene: A fairly tall Indian guy with curly hair playing guitar. A crowd cheering and humming to his song.

Nidhi couldn't get her eyes off this gentleman performing music. She was sitting at the drinks table sipping on her whisky. Once the crowd dispersed, the guy came and sat next to Nidhi. He asked the bartender for his drink.

"There's something magical in your voice!" Nidhi praised him.

"Well, let us call it tragic." The guy chuckled.

"Nidhi, by the way!"

"I am Mayank! Please meet you Nidhi."

16

This One's for Love

by Nitya Saini

Mehu, please bring me two test tubes and a volumetric flask. And, do it fast." Asked, rather ordered Mrs. Vyas.

"*Mehwish*! My name is Mehwish."

She hated it when someone called her *Mehu*. Mrs. Sharma was the first to call her favorite lab assistant by this nickname, and soon afterward three other teachers started calling her that. She couldn't understand what was suddenly wrong with those people. The mere sound of that word Me—she couldn't even bear to say it in her head—she loathed that word. It brought back memories, harrowing memories, she would do anything to forget those, only if it was in her control. Her palms began to get clammy. Her head felt dizzy. A crippling fear ran through her body.

"Mehwish, I asked you to do something. Where are you lost these days?" Mrs. Vyas snapped at her.

"I'm sorry, Mrs. Vyas. I'll get those for you." Answered Mehwish nervously.

She had been, indeed, lost in her thoughts these days. October—it was something with this month, that all her thoughts played nasty games with her head. She hadn't been feeling like herself lately. At this particular instant, her mind was flooded with chaos and restlessness, but she didn't let her work suffer. She had no excuse for her absent-mindedness. Not any that she wanted to discuss with anyone. She handed her the items as soon as she could and quickly walked out of the lab.

The clock showed 3:45 pm. It had been more than an hour since she reached her home. Usually, she would fall asleep as soon as she laid on her bed. But these days were not like the rest. As she was lying with her eyes closed, every moment flashed through her eyes. Her past haunted her. She flitted across the bed, trying hard to fall asleep. Yet, she couldn't. It was this day, 14 years ago, when her life changed completely.

For the majority of her life, Mehwish had known herself to be shy and aloof. However, she wasn't always this way. She used to be a cheerful girl, who didn't leave her mother alone for a minute. Little troublemaker. But the innocence in her eyes saved her from any penalty. Her mother was her favorite, loving, and nurturing woman. Her father though was a janitor by day, and a mean old alcoholic at night, who would spare no mercy to her mother. The sound of her mother's cries is still audible to her ears. She was only 6 years old when her mother killed herself. After her mother's death, his father's new target was his little girl. Those innocent eyes, that could melt anyone's heart with just a glance, couldn't shake that man of stone. He cussed her in every way possible. She always believed or wanted to believe that it was only his circumstances that made him so cruel. He wasn't bad at heart, which changed eventually.

October 8, 2003, at 8:01 p.m.—this date and time are etched upon her mind. It was the day of her 10th birthday. She suffered too much for such a tender age, but that day she was happy. Happiness, though, never lasted too long for her. Just like every other day, her father came home drunk. His eyes glittered differently that day. He called her, "*Mehu*, come here." He made her sit in his lap and touched her in every possible way a girl should never be touched. She wanted to resist, but her limbs froze. For a moment she couldn't believe her father could do this to her. She never felt so weak in her entire life. Finally, she gathered all her courage, pushed her father away, and ran straight into her room. She was hunted down by her father on different occasions. Sometimes, beaten up mercilessly. Her father gave her scars even though time is incapable of healing.

On her 13th birthday, she decided that it was enough for him. Her decision was stern and nothing could stop her. Except, she felt a hand strongly pulling her inside, as she was escaping her way out through the window. Her father understood all her motives, and as *responsible* a father as he was, he couldn't let her young daughter wander around in dark on those lonely streets. They got into a fight. She used all her strength to let go of his father. But he was too strong. In the heat of the moment, she picked up her father's bottle of cheap whiskey and smashed it forcefully on his father's skull. She saw her father fall slowly on the floor. He took his last breath that day. She was frightened for her life. She couldn't think of anything but to run away from that home, and never come back. Her father must be either buried by one of her neighbours, or he rots in that very house. She still didn't know that. Neither did she want to. No one cared. Her father was a nobody, anyway.

A young girl of 13 with nowhere to go, Mehwish wandered for days for food and shelter. She finally found refuge in the house of a woman of late fifties, a chemistry teacher who lived alone and was looking for someone to help her with the chores. She passed away 5 years ago. Since then, she has taken care of her house.

Her eyes welled up as she dwelled deep into the dungeons of her past. She didn't want to go any further. A tear rolled down her cheek. She wiped it off and closed her eyes, with the hope that maybe these visions wouldn't disturb her anymore. She was finally able to fall asleep.

***

Kaavish arrived at his date's house at 7:40 in the evening. 20 minutes prior to the decided time. His excitement knew no bounds. It was the first time she invited him to her house. They had only gone out twice before, but he just couldn't stop thinking about her. He had never met a girl so elegant and confident as *Ibtida*. There was something in her hazel eyes that took his heart away. He stood up straight, took a deep breath, and knocked at her door.

"Hey! Someone is early. I had a surprise planned for you. Can you wait for a minute honey?", said her date.

For a moment, he couldn't take his eyes off her. Her red dress beautifully accentuated her curves. The innocence with which she requested him melted his heart straightaway. He couldn't say no to her even if he tried. After a few minutes, she let him in. Scented candles and red roses graced that night's party. She turned on the stereo and gracefully walked towards him. They embraced and danced to the rhythm. She tried hard to hide it, but she couldn't. The way she looked into Kaavish's eyes—it gave her away. She wanted more, so much more that she wanted to do to him. He was also the happiest to have the girl of her fancy in her arms. But then suddenly, he started to run out of breath. His vision blurred. His face had gone pale. He was trying his best to stand straight but within a minute, he was lying unconscious on the ground. Finally, she was relieved. Usually, it doesn't take more than 15 minutes for GHB to do its magic. She was starting to worry that this time she would fail, but just like always her plan worked perfectly fine. The surprise had only begun. After all, you don't drug anyone without a reason. Ibtida unbuttoned his pants and gently slid them down. Her eyes scintillated and slowly a sinister grin lighted her face. This year she found her prey after a lot of efforts, her excitement was justified. It's finally about to go down—she was eager.

In the beginning, she slowly ran the knife through his scrotum. Then within a single blow, she performed her favorite venture. *Blam*! Blood splashed all over her face. She held his bloodied penis in her hand and stared at it for a minute. Her prized possession. Then ruthlessly slashed it into more pieces. She enjoyed this bit the most. Lucky for her, she always covered the floor with plastic sheets first. Hence, cleaning up was never a big deal for her. She wrapped the body in those sheets, shoved it into her car, and carried it to the plot nearby. *This one's for love*—she said as he was bid his farewell and buried into the ground. Living away from the city had its advantages—she thought as she drove away. Transporting those heavy men had always been a little difficult. Even the skinny ones felt heavier. But it wasn't even close to something she wasn't capable of. She had accomplished her act.

For the remainder of the year, Ibtida lived in a secluded cottage in Amman. She didn't like to be around people. Every October she would take the time to visit her native home in

India for a month. Her father's home. He traumatized her to a degree that cannot even be expressed in words. She always wanted to avenge him but couldn't. He died long ago. So, she came up with a plan to ease her soul. She would torture every guy that in any way reminded her of her father.

Her vile adventures began 5 years back. Since then, she has fallen in love with 8 guys. She was aware of at least 10 ways to kill them in one go. But first, she liked to see them tremble with pain. As the wonder drug made them helpless enough to help themselves, she could easily perform the deed, watching them lie powerless on the floor. Although half of October was left, she was satisfied, well, too tired to hunt down another man and was planning to leave for Amman in a few days.

***

It was a new day. Mehwish was feeling much better today. Well, chiefly because Shahryar joined the school again. Her heart always had a soft spot for him. She liked how respectful he was towards every person, especially women. He was a very handsome man, with eyes that pierce right through one's heart in just a look. Since the day she saw him, she always wanted to talk to him. But being the shy girl that she was, she couldn't say anything more than a "hello" when he came in front of her. Seeing him at the school that day, she was extremely happy.

"Mehwish! How are you? It's so great to finally see someone I know. Most of the staff has changed now", said Shahryar while shaking her hand.

She was glad that he hadn't forgotten her in those 3 years.

"I'm good. And you?"

"I'm great. Feels so good to be back. Hey, I'll catch up with you after school. Got some important work to do. See you."

When the school departed, he was standing at the school gate. He waved at her. At first, she couldn't believe that he was waiting for her. He had never done that. Earlier he didn't even notice her. She was excited and nervous at the same time. Her focus was mainly on not blurting out anything that made her seem nervous.

"The city has changed a lot in these years. Most of my friends have moved away. I don't even know where to buy groceries from."

"I know some places. I can also help you with setting up your new home if you want." Those were the greatest number of words she had ever said to him. She was surprised.

"That'd be great. I could use some help", he was pleased to know that someone was willing to give him a helping hand.

Besides, assisting in helping with his home, they began spending a lot of time together. In school too they were mostly with each other whenever both of them weren't working. They talked a lot, about science, mythology, and simply about what was happening in each other's lives. This was the most she had spoken to someone in a long time now. It had been more than a month since they got so close. Lately, she hadn't been wallowing much in her misery. She felt happy when she was him. She wanted to tell him how she felt, everything, but she was too scared. She couldn't even bear the thought of losing him. Apart from that, she wasn't sure if he felt the same way.

The next day had dawned. It was just a plain ordinary day, until this one moment. Shahryar asked her out. It was the first time she was going out with someone. He felt the same way—

she was jumping with joy. At 6 pm he picked her up for their date. Mehwish looked beautiful. She wanted to look her best, after all, it was her first date. He was wearing a black chikankari kurta. It reminded her of her father. He also wore one similar to his. For a moment, she was drawn to her horrible past, but she pulled herself back soon afterward. He is nothing like him…she told herself.

They reached the venue around 8:30. The food, the ambiance, and of course the company…everything was amazing. After their dinner, he walked her home. It was only this very night that she realized his gait resembled a lot of her father. Every time she thought of her father, a menacing fear took hold of her. Something so powerful, she wanted to throw up. She spaced out.

"I had a great time tonight", he said smilingly.

"Yeah, me too", she woke up from her delirium.

"So, I'll see you at school tomorrow."

He was about to leave for his place, but he didn't move an inch even. It was pretty obvious that he wanted to stay a little longer. Then suddenly she held his hand, pulled him close, and kissed him hard.

Shahryar was startled. His eyes were wide open.

"Woah! I… I never thought you would be the first one to make this move. This is so unlike you. I don't mean I didn't like it. Sorry, I meant…"

"Well, sometimes you ought to change your tune. You can come inside if you want", she said and kissed him even harder. He was inside her house now. She pushed him onto the bed and just like that they started caressing. What am I doing and how am I so good at all this? She thought as she paused for a bit. She couldn't believe herself. Her body was never so graceful. Her hands were touching all the right places. It didn't seem like she was with a man for the first time. She had never felt so confident in her entire life. Yet she was utterly confused. She wasn't thinking about it up until that moment. Even at that time, she didn't know what she was doing. It felt as if someone else took control of her body. This was indeed unlike her.

"Mehwish listen."

He called her quite a few times, but she didn't respond. After being ignored many times, he shook her up and stopped.

"Mehwish. I think…"

"Call me *Ibtida*."

"You must be thirsty. Let me get you some water", she continued.

"I didn't know you had a nickname too, and I think I should leave now", he was puzzled. Not that he didn't like any of that, he just really needed to go. But she couldn't let him go just like that. She wanted to make the most of that opportunity. But only that night she decided that it would be the last day of his life. Just as he was about to turn to get the glass of water, she struck him forcefully with a rod. Within a minute, he collapsed on the floor.

She was all ready to perform the ritual. He was Ibtida's guest now. She had encountered him a few times before. Although only for a brief time, one day she even talked to him in the market. He seemed like a nice and simple man. Up until she saw him walk away, it bore a striking resemblance to his father's. But it was too late when she realized that. He had gone far away. It was that day when she decided she would hunt him down whenever she saw him next. And call it coincidence or fate, he was standing right outside his door.

Just when she was halfway in the act, the knife fell from her hand. She screamed with fear. How could I do this to the man I love? Mehwish said out loud. She couldn't even think of doing it in her wildest dreams. She didn't understand why she had a knife in her hand. She tried to wake him up, but he didn't respond. He was not breathing. Never in her life, she had been so petrified. She saw her love lie dead on the ground; it took a few minutes for her to accept. She was still traumatized by the fact that she killed her father. And now Shahryar. The man she loved more than anything. She went numb. Her mind was not capable of processing anything anymore.

Suddenly a hostile force took over her. She picked up the knife and resumed what she left. After 10 seconds, she stopped. Why'd she picked up the knife, she couldn't understand. At one moment she wanted him dead, and in the other, she felt immense pain of loss. She couldn't understand what was happening with her and why she'd done that, but she knew, in that instant with certainty, that she was the one behind it. She had murdered him. It took some minutes for her to realize that something within herself was making her do it. She felt so guilty, she wanted to die too. She couldn't bear to look at him that way. Something was stopping her. She was hearing voices. Loud and clear. Evil, helpless—all kinds of voices. At one minute she was the timid and defenseless Mehwish and in another, the cunning and wicked Ibtida.

Her heart broke every time she realized that she was fighting with herself. And that it was her body, but it was inhabited by someone else too. Someone, although a part of her, yet completely different. Someone she couldn't even imagine to be, not even in her worst nightmares. Yet she was so many beings. She understood if she kept Ibtida alive she would only cause more misery in the world. Ibtida needed to die. Every shred of her needed to vanish. She didn't want to live with her. She didn't want anyone to find out about her. Her heart was growing heavy, but in that very moment, nothing seemed more right to her. She would never be able to live with all this pain. She stood still for some time, wiped her tears off, and set fire to the whole place, and herself with it. Everything burned to the ground. She looked at Shahryar, his body was burning up in flames. Mehwish looked at his face, which had still not caught fire, just for one last time. It was the final goodbye until she took her last breath and burnt to the ground.

17

The Unheard Voice

by Mansi Gupta

I think it's the medicines. C'mon, you can't deny that they don't F*** with your mind" claimed Yogi, a 24-year-old tattoo-sleeved student who was training under Jayshree for a certification course in Counselling and Psychotherapy.

"I don't know what it is, but honestly I feel like I don't know the man anymore. Like, is he even my father? He has changed so much since he was diagnosed with anxiety and depression last year," replied Sanjana who overused the word 'like.' She was younger than Yogi.

The tiny classroom of 18 students, waited for them to end their prattle, Miss Jayshree had entered the room and she was waiting patiently to begin her lecture. Jayshree was 42, separated, but loved to flaunt her 'mangalsutra' (A neck-piece worn by an Indian woman which is equivalent to a wedding ring) with the rare sarees she wore. If asked why, she would nonchalantly respond, "I love how it looks on me. Just because we don't live together, doesn't mean I have to give away my favourite piece of jewellery." Was there room for reconciliation? Well, it seems like the therapist needs her therapist to answer that.

"Urmm…" Jayshree cleared her throat to make her presence felt in the room. The room! With one tiny window at the back end that was completely blocked by a towering coconut tree almost like it was peeping in the room like a nosy, gossip starved neighbour, blocking any sunlight that could have entered this dim lit property, the room was not a 'classroom.' It always had an odour of a peculiar oil that Anil was generously using every morning on his head to grow back his lost tresses. Anil was Jayshree's accountant slash admin cleaner. He had a corner with a bulky monitor and the slowest CPU that existed in Mumbai, India. Anil would randomly sing some Maharashtrian songs while the class was on and would have to be reminded that his headphones don't make 'his own' voice soundproof. The students loved this setup.

"Sorry, ma'am," said Yogi just as he figured that everyone was a part of their 'not so silent conversation.'

"Is there anything that you would like to talk about Sanjana?" asked Jayshree with those empathetic eyes that made everyone want to talk to her.

"Ma'am, I have told you about my father. I feel his condition is deteriorating. Why can't we stop these medications when we know that they have side effects?! Why do people even allow these psychiatrists to prescribe medicines?" She sounded irate and exasperated.

"Pull a chair. Sit. Let me read out something to you. Seems like today's session will have to be about Counsellors vs Psychiatrists" smiled Jayshree.

She called out to Anil and requested him to find her, 'The Then Diary.' Diaries were a sensitive subject with Jayshree.

Her ex-husband would find out why she was upset because she would journal the entire fight down. Verbatim. Her diaries have always been up to date and that helped her track her movements, her sessions, and her appointments extremely well. No wonder Jayshree thinks of computers as a menace.

Dusting the long-forgotten diary that Anil had just handed her over she said, "Let me read this out to you. You may take notes now. Questions in the end please."

Jayshree began:

16th July 2018

"I have to file the patient data but honestly I am so restless today that all I want is a long run. I met Diya again. It has been 3 months since we started her therapy. She responds so well to the traditional Psychotherapy sessions, that I don't understand where am I going wrong?

But something tells me that this case is not what I imagined it to be. Is it her? Is it my separation? Am I mixing my feelings with this case? Every time I meet her, I am compelled to revisit my therapist.

Diya is a 34-year-old, recently divorced, extremely anxious girl who was diagnosed with depression and anxiety after her divorce. She was a patient of Psychiatrist, Dr. Khanna."

Jayashree realized that she was trembling. Her body found it difficult to call him that. Dr. Suyansh Khanna whom she referred to as 'Swe' since she first met him 11 years ago, was her ex-husband. They have maintained a professional relationship but just his name and the memories rush back. Composing herself quickly, Jayshree got back to the diary.

"The poor girl was drugged by Dr. Khanna." He thought she needed the heavy dose to get through her divorce. So many medicines just to keep her functioning! These were my initial assumptions.

Note for next session:

Remind Diya to keep practicing deep meditation using my audio clips.

20th July 2018

This is the first time we met twice a week. Diya looked apprehensive about her new job. She didn't even tell me that she was looking for a change of job! I thought of asking her.

"I didn't know you were looking for a job," were my exact words to her. But she seemed offended by the question.

"You don't know a lot about me!! We meet once in 15 days. The other 14 days, I have thoughts too, just FYI," she said angrily.

"You know you are welcome here. Anytime. I told her reassuringly. You just need to call like you did today." But my sentence was interrupted.

"You know, I am not here for me today. I am here for Jwaala!" said Diya with her voice quite raised now.

Diya shared a home with her mother near Andheri station. She had mentioned that her mother had partial paralysis. Having Diya around was helpful but her mother had nurses who did a great job; is what Diya had informed me.

Jwaala is their next-door neighbour. Diya and Jwaala had connected very well since Diya's divorce. Jwaala had turned 8 last week. Diya had shared with me the beautiful poem she wrote for her. Jwaala had asked her for 'a bat.' She wanted to break open her father's skull is what she confided in Diya.

Jwaala's parents were always arguing about something or the other. Her mother would come to the stairwell, (where Diya and Jwaala often sat at the end of the day discussing how each one spent their day) she would grab Diya and mutter, "Sitting again with this divorcee. Why did she have to enter our lives?! Stay away from my home." Jwaala's mom hated Diya. Diya empathized with Jwaala, but she was very disturbed about these thoughts in the head of an 8-year-old.

"You have to help me." She was begging me that day. "I'll pay you separately for Jwaala's therapy. I tried to explain to her that, as outsiders, we have a limited role to play. I can't go to their house and ask for help for the child. Child services in our country too are limited for the underprivileged and I can't send her to an orphanage when both her parents are alive, educated, and working!"

Diya seemed very restless.

She only spoke about how abusive Jwaala's mother could get and the words she often used. 'This home breaker. This selfish bitch had to come into our lives.' Jwaala would hear these words and hide behind the staircase. She would only return when her mother was no longer around.'

When I first met Diya in April 2018, she would only talk about how trapped her medication made her feel. She said that the reason she came to therapy was only to stop those medicines. Convincing her for a lighter dose was a tough job for me! Diya didn't have any children of her own. She was divorced within a couple of years of being married. 'We fell out of love' was her only response to my probing about her marriage.

The first few months, I realized that she isn't ready to talk about her marriage. So, I strengthened her with various meditation techniques and visualization aids that helped her quit the meds and be free. But things seemed different now. I felt like I needed to put her back on the medication to calm her a bit. It's always a tough call for a counsellor.

I had contacted Dr. Khanna's office and asked for some meds to calm her for tonight. He suggested a lighter dose of her previous meds for this current period. It was the need of the hour and Diya luckily agreed.

I told Diya that I would pick up her medicines and drop them at her place the next day as I didn't want her to go through the anxiety of the psychiatrist's office.

Her house was on my way to the clinic. But I could sense her discomfort inviting me home.

'Unusual' I thought.

I promised Diya to find a solution for Jwaala and also to see her the next day with her meds.

21st July 2018

I waited for quite long at Starbucks as discussed. I couldn't see her. I called. Her phone was switched off. I don't know why I thought... Let me drop these meds at her place! She needs them urgently and she will understand my over interference. Maybe, If I am lucky. I will get to meet Jwaala.

I met Jwaala...

I asked the watchman about their floor and explained that I was her doctor. He said last month too her mother had called the doctor home. I presumed it was for her 'paralysis.'

I walked towards the house. There were two houses on each floor. I looked at the other one and saw a lock outside. Maybe Jwaala and her parents were away I thought to myself.

I saw the staircase, it was dimly lit. I imagined little Jwaala confiding here in Diya.

I rang the bell...

A woman in her early 60s answered the door. I said, "I am looking for Diya. Do I have the wrong address?"

The woman with her well-blow-dried hair and kaftan replied, "No, my dear please come in. I'll just call her. She is in her room sleeping. I think she had too much of her medicines. She does that often and we have to call the doctor home."

I looked puzzled. Too much information! Was I being confused with someone else?

I am Jayshree, Diya's counsellor, I said and you are?

"Oh! I didn't know she had a counsellor. I thought you are another psychiatrist. She has changed many psychiatrists but counsellor! That's the first I am hearing of it."

"Did she tell you that she overdoses on her meds now and then? Initially, we thought she is suicidal, but later I realized she just seeks attention after her divorce. Such a charming boy Rajeev was. I still miss him, you know. I tell all my friends, given a choice, I would have adopted him and let go of this angry, psychotic, just like her father."

Diya had told me that her father had passed away a year before her divorce. So, I again interrupted the indulging, talkative lady who seemed to have no boundaries and said, "I am sorry for your loss. Are you one of her aunt's?"

"What loss?"

"The only loss I have, is to deal with this father-daughter duo."

She was interrupted by a man who I assumed was her husband and then she said something that made me look at life a lot differently...

Jayashree shut her diary and looked at her students.

The woman said, "This is my husband John, Jwaala's father."

I looked at her perplexed and said, "I am sorry???"

"I am Diya's mother and this is her father."

The paralysis of the mother and the death of the father baffled me. I nervously asked, "Why did you say Jwaala?"

"Oh, I am so sorry..." she replied.

"When Diya was young around 7 or 8, we gave her a nickname- Jwaala. Her anger cannot be managed! Not by me at least. Whenever I call her Jwaala it's a reminder for me that she is saying things only because she is angry. That woman is tough I tell you! She would rather spend hours sitting outside the house on that bloody staircase, talking to herself but wouldn't tell me the truth about her divorce. Rajeev, her ex, confided in me and told me all about her erratic behaviour, her medicines, her overdose, her attention-seeking behaviour, and all the spying."

"It's like different people live in her head!"

Suddenly, we realized that someone else was in the room.

We turned our heads. I could now feel the shiver in my inner thighs. The sweat beads down my spine.

I turned and said, "Hi Diya!"

Diya looked at me with a blank stare and told her mother in a very childish voice, "Who is this aunty Mumma?"

"Jwaala, have you been seeing a counsellor?" her mom asked.

"What's a counsellor?" Diya sounded like a young girl about 8.

The medicines fell off my hands.

She looked at me with a look in her eyes that I can never forget.

That day, life reminded me of the difference between psychiatry and counselling! I know you have a million questions students, let's begin.

18

Can You Hear My Conscience?

by Dewni De Silva

The waves crash and bombard the rocks near the shore. I try to walk past it, quickening my pace, the wet sand drawing in my feet to slow down my pace. Each breath I drew made me taste the saltiness at the back of my throat, heightening the sense of petulance. Today was a perfect day, yet the sun kept attacking with all her rays and I couldn't fight his brutality.

When I finally sit by the shore, Ameen too sits down next to me, his body drenched, weary, and looking pale as a ghost. My heart aches at the sight of him when he looks directly at me, trying to say something.

"You seem shaken." He says.

"You can't be here," I utter to myself, almost inaudible. Closing my eyes, I feel a sense of peace, drawing each breath with confidence.

I close my eyes.

"This is just a conscience."

Before.

My room was missing its door. The skies were open to rain, suiting the mood of the city of decay. The place was heated up to the extent that sweat trickled down my back, forcing me to adjust to the abhorrent smell that possessed the house. Outside, the vomitous ordure radiates around the whole place. The hijab I've been wearing for 4 straight days looks olive-colour, mixed with the dust and the sweat of the atmosphere of Homs. Syria was in absolute shackles. When the opposite political parties went haywire for the power-driven city, they killed most civilians and protestors and set fire to all rationality and freedom, forcing a systematic revolution, nothing less than another holocaust. The Americans invaded Syria, giving upper hand to war, the only underlying motive to sell more weapons.

I'm a Syrian girl, named after her late grandmother – Afif. It meant I was a simple and a chaste daughter. I absolutely loved how my mother combed her hair to the side, I loved how she wore her patched-up dress, covering her ankle. Always so neat. After she died during the bombing, I always keep her comb beside my already-broken mirror. It reminded me of her smile whenever I asked her to style my hair instead of hers.

'Hurry the news is on' Ameen screams.

We huddle together, and I see how Ameen is seated, one knee crooked and seems disconnected from his body. The images on the news however were more appalling to me. the blaring sirens, decrepit buildings are the only documentaries the screen has to offer. Syria hasn't ever looked this bad.

My father spits whatever he was chewing. He is undoubtedly feebler today than yesterday. His once black hair is now fully white, mocking his age. He held on to Ameen, his eyes still lingering on the screen.

'These haters' Father lashes his knife out while Ameen seems unbothered by all the turmoil. "What can we do, Ameen?" My father speaks to him but isn't exactly directed at him to answer. Ameen, 12 years of age, yet so thoughtful, doesn't respond.

"We don't have any food," I say. I contemplate about how wrong I was to remind myself about food, knowing that stepping outside is a suicide mission. There were protesters everywhere, keeping an eye out for anyone that moves within the city.

My father suddenly stands up, his face still scowling at the screen. He starts to walk towards me with a slow gate, dragging his left leg on the cement floor. My heart pounded when I realized what was happening.

"Take-care of Ameen," he says. There was something so desperate about him in his eyes. His walk, how he looked around. My heart races even more when he exits from the door, not daring to look back at us for a second time.

After.

I grip Ameen's hand, signalling him to stop squirming. He fidgets and scrapes my hand, yearning to let loose. I look at him and slap his face, saying "They can hear you," through my gritted teeth.

My feelings were replaced with a new form of pique. I randomly begin to tug at my hair, as if I feel something squirming on my head. I imagined it growing, clawing its way through my skin, and absorbing all my senses. I felt like someone enclasped their hands around me, stifling me, making me do things I don't intend to.

The veil we were hiding behind was a bad cover. It had holes which could fit my whole fist. The curtain beneath the veil, once cheery and full of colours, now took the shades of death-colours. My ears listened vigilantly to any motion in our house. There was someone lurking out there in the dark, I was sure.

We have to keep moving, my conscience screamed and tore at my notions like a parasite. Crawling and digging into my skull, planting seeds of hatred, seeds of fear, replacing my rationality. I place my hands firmly on my knee, not just to support my ruined self, but to keep my legs from shaking.

The footsteps were ever so close that I felt like someone right behind us. With my heart pounding out of my chest, I turn my head slowly towards where the sound was coming from. I stare at the distance, dubiously.

I advise Ameen to not make a commotion. We can't trade lives here.

Before.

"What are we going to do?" Ameen asks me, his body tensed. I on the other hand was composed, trying to think of ways I could save us from these ruins. Every inch of my body aches for him, the weight of the world resting on my hunched shoulder.

I caress his hair, telling him some of my happy memories. "I'll always look after you," I say, even though my conscience blames me for making promises I can't keep a grasp of.

"Isn't he coming back?" He cries.

"Is he coming back?" Now he's screaming. His voice breaks when he says my name as if I were to blame. "Are you telling me we are left here to die, with no food, no place to sleep, do we have to hide every time someone…"

"Put a sock on it," I say, my nerves about to test me. I shrink to the floor lifelessly, thinking about how I'm supposed to support Ameen without a father. I could hear mild screams in the distance, but I know there's no one around for miles. I've been hearing the noises since the first attack, how the floor seemed to not be strong enough to hold everyone in Homs. How it shook for what seemed like an eternity, forcing us to crawl underneath our beds, praying the roof won't betray us.

I remember how mother was motionless near my bed. Her head bent at this odd angle, her eyes wide open, staring at nothing. She was still clutching her dress, almost as she was dead.

After.

"I hear someone," Ameen whispers.

"Who's there?" My voice echoes through the hallway, through the broken glasses. We weren't alone.

Then I heard a click.

We turn our heads, puzzled where it's coming from. "Don't shout." Ameen begged. He hung on to my niqab, the hem of it now loose from the dress. "Don't kill us Afif."

A tall figure approached us, setting out the gunshots. It happened too fast that both Ameen and I ducked with fear, our ears ringing, eardrums feeling bruised and attacked.

"Who are you!" I screamed clutching to my dear life. I felt so helpless that I remembered the look in my mother's eyes just before she passed. I saw the final glance my father did before he closed the door behind him. I'm looking at Ameen's muted screams, unable to help him.

Someone lifts me from where I was lying, on to my feet.

'Hyenas' the man spits into my face.

I struggle to reach the ground, but he holds me from my neck, his grip tightening. His eyes seemed to jut out from his face, the scars on his face make no room for clear brown-skin. He was clearly not his senses. Holding the gun in his right hand, he points it to my forehead.

"Hyenas will shoot, but I'll shoot you first."

"Wha-what do you want?"

He lowers his gun and points it towards my bag. It had everything we stored.

Shaking my head vigorously, "no way," I mutter. 'Ameen doesn't give the bag' I rebel, trying to get away from his grasp. He abruptly releases me and goes after the bag.

"Run, Ameen," I scream. But I watched the mad man, tear the bag away from my brother's hands and point the gun, accusing us.

"If you follow me I'll butcher you." He said, taking one step back.

Ameen looked at me and shook his head slightly. "Don't."

We had food there. It was the last of the supplies.

We're doomed.

Before.

My brain was numb by then. After what seemed like hours, I gained the energy to sit next to her. I checked her pulse and was surprised to feel her energy so faintly. She raised her cold hands, motioned me to take the chunk of brick that lay directly on top of her feet.

I smile at her, ever so warmly. I kiss her forehead and look at her.

She kept grabbing my hand, with the strength left within her, pleading with her eyes to move the bricks in any possible way.

But I don't.

I just stare at her, my lips pursed. Poised in a way I could almost see her soul detaching from her body.

I don't do anything.

I reached for a cement stone that seemed to fit in my hands.

"You can let go," I say, hitting her head as swiftly as I could, offering her a less painful death.

And I'd never forget the look on her face.

After.

I felt the anger rise up in my throat, that if I spit it out, I'd see black. In my head was this ineffable void, sucking my thoughts like a blackhole. In that blackhole I see memories of my mother, how shockingly disable her entire body was. Instead of trying to move, she planted her faith in me.

"I told you to run," I say.

"The man had a gun," he says. He sits down once again, on the uneven floor, nervously touching his shirt, wiping his sweat, rubbing his palms, and licking his dry lips.

I sway my head to this monotonous rhythm in my head that's been playing ever since the bombing. It was like a lull that gambled with my head. Suddenly I feel like tugging at my air, overwhelmed by insanity and pain. I pinch the bridge of my nose, taking effort to fight back exasperation. When I close my eyes I see my mother staring, her image raided my thoughts. They crawl on me like it owns me. They caress my hair like it knows what I'll do next. It suppresses my veins, choking my throat and stabbing me – piercing my sanity.

We have to get out.

After.

We walked till our feet knotted and blisters ached. Ameen's shoulders were slumped forward, making him look shorter. I had nothing to carry but myself. I wanted my bag, the food in it, a water drop that would suffice my parched mouth.

"Is that the sound of the sea?" Ameen asks.

Ameen runs towards the waves, trampling the gooey sand with his feet. The sea glistened to the myriad sunrays, such a happy feeling. Deep down, I knew I had Ameen to hold on to. I watched him step on the shallow end of the coast, calling me.

I felt a new form of relief, looking at Ameen, now bobbing his head to the rhythm of the water. The sand was hot, so I ran towards the water, forcing my feet to entangle with water. The blisters on my feet sighed with relief at the feel of ocean goodness.

"What can we do Afif?" He asks, sounding exactly like father. The back of my eyes burn and my hands shake relentlessly. To hide this, I grabbed his hands and embraced him.

"Mother wasn't dead when I found her," I say.

"What?"

I don't know what's worse, not feeling any emotion or not wanting to feel any. Without hesitation I grip him by the back of his neck, pushing down under the calm water that rose above his head. His arms flayed, dangled in so many angles, reaching for my dress and pulling me down. I tighten my right hand around his hands, much confidently straining him, tiring him to his death. When he tried to lift himself above those cruel tides that drowned him, challenging their strength, the waves in return, drowned him further, my job was simply to keep him down.

The fight receded and there was so much silence. His arms stopped with no warning, didn't move no more, neither did his body. The dead-weight looked like a peaceful thing to watch, lulling to the waves that tossed and turned.

I slowly take my hand, pushing him into the sea, hoping the waves wouldn't bring him back.

<h1 style="text-align:center">19</h1>

<h1 style="text-align:center">One More Time</h1>

by Ranjna Gopal

If there was a problem that needed solving CR33D was the one. One text and problem solved, provided you were willing to pay the price.

Three in one night!! That was a record even for CR33D. She smiled to herself as she thought over the events of the evening. From the moment she entered the charity gala to the last assignment.

Tonight was indeed a special one, her honey-brown eyes sparkled, and a playful smile danced at her lips as she remembered seeing Donelly seniors expression as she had caressed his face while plunging the dagger straight into his chest, just slightly to the left and breaking the tip. She recalled the irritation she felt when she realized Mrs. Donelly was standing behind her mouth ready to scream. Oh well, a straight cut to her wrinkly ivory neck had shut her up. The piece de resistance was Donelly Junior who she had met on the stairs on her way down. Now she openly smiled, it was just too easy to flirt and guide him to one of the many bedrooms while his parents bled out. The idiot had actually thought she was interested!!! Too easy, she began to giggle as his shocked face crept into her mind. The look as he realized she had sliced his jugular while caressing his back. Oh, they had all made it too simple. Like father, like son, the analogy made her laugh out loud. Yes, this is why she was the best. She knew she had a long and interesting career ahead of her.

The woman sat quietly in her car waiting, she knew it wouldn't be long but the waiting was making her nervous.

The worst thing about these night shifts was that she never knew how long she'd be working. Her coffee had gone cold and had that scummy foam on top that only comes from obscure gas station coffee machines. Time was dragging making her edgy and impatient.

The quinoa and chicken salad she had devoured earlier had barely made a dent in her stomach, the craving for a nice juicy big mac flooded her senses. Her stomach growled like a wounded wildebeest reminding her that this low cholesterol diet her doctor had put her on had no plus factors whatsoever. Including distracting her from the job at hand.

Katie's mind strayed to the pile of marking she had left by the computer, she had known taking this second job would take her away from the work she adored.

Teaching at the exclusive school where the rich, famous, and politicians sent their children certainly paid the bills but this job was for a future she could only dream of.

She wanted this night to hurry up and finish. It was 01.25 and she was still waiting.

Fighting to keep her eyes open she reached for the glove compartment to find the energy drink she had left there earlier. "Come on Katie! FOCUS!" This was taking too long, she checked her account one last time, the row of zeros shocking her back to the moment.

A movement caught her peripheral vision, finally, the back entrance of the club door opened.

The woman staggered out propped up by what Katie presumed was her security guard. What a waste of a human being and with so much power. The woman removed her shoes, laughing coarsely and slurring Katie couldn't make out what she said but it didn't matter anyway. To think someone like this could destroy life for so many with a little budget cut. She wondered if the shoes were Louboutin or Jimmy Choo.

What was wrong with her today? She only had a window of around 30 seconds to complete her task, no time to swoon over the woman's shoes or the expensive cut of her clothes.

Katie felt that familiar rush of adrenaline mixed with guilt. Silently she opened the car door, ready, aim and release. The kunai flew seamlessly through the air, like a hot knife through butter. The shocked look on the woman's face as she began wildly grabbing at her neck clearly visible in the reflection of the vehicle she was waiting to enter. As she fell to the floor Katie slipped back into her hybrid. Tick tock time was ticking, she glanced in the rear-view mirror, a satisfied smile crept across her face. That had to be one of her best, straight through the neck, oh yes, she felt pride in her craft. That moment when life left the mark was pure bliss. Unseen, unheard she was gone, thank god for the invention of eco-friendly engines.

The strange gurgling noise alerted the woman's security, his eyes widened as he saw the blood pouring from her neck. The tip of the blade peeking almost coyly from the front of her neck.

Panic set in as he called for assistance.

"Ambulance, stab wound to the throat."

He knew it was futile, she had stood no chance the blade had penetrated straight through. What had he missed? Where had it come from? He looked around wildly seeking a clue, anything, but there was nothing. What about her son? He heard the distant wail of sirens as thoughts rushed through his head. What the hell just happened? But most of all the cold dark knowledge that this had happened on his watch.

The drive home was always slow, this was her last job and it had been the hardest. Maybe she was getting too old for this, tonight was the first time she had hesitated.

That big mac wormed its way back into her head. Why the hell was she always so hungry after a job? She pulled into her driveway, tomorrow this life would be over, as looked in the fridge for something vaguely healthy she still couldn't shake that moment of hesitation. This assignment didn't sit well with Katie, maybe because even though the woman was a complete waste of space she was a mother. She shook herself as if to rid herself of the guilt and breathed deeply. A job was a job nothing more, nothing less. She crawled into bed overcome with exhaustion.

Morning came with bright sunlight pouring through the window, Katie rose slowly, this job had changed her in some way. She showered quickly and dressed in the familiar uniform of St. Mary's school. Walking into the halls she had walked for the last 3 years she felt a sadness she hadn't expected to feel. As she entered her classroom the chatter of the children became deafening.

"Ma'am Christian isn't here."

"Everyone's saying his mum is dead."

Hearing them say, it sent an ice-cold shiver through her and she became conscious of the empty space where her star pupil Christian James normally sat.

The burn at the back of her throat surprised her and the words that came from her mouth felt alien as though a stranger was speaking to them.

"Children we must not gossip. I need to go see Sister Theresa."

She excused herself and walked slowly to the head office, her heels clicking in the way that only teachers do. Those Louboutins popped into her head again.

The meeting with Sister Theresa was swift. "Take as much time as you need." That was all the Sister said.

Katie said a quick goodbye to the children explaining she needed to go away for a while and began the long drive. Flights were booked and all documents ready four more hours and this life would be over. Katie Mcgee would no longer exist.

Just one quick stop along the way. She began to relax, she loved the fields along the way to the only place she had really ever called home.

The blue door of the cottage was already opening and he ran out before she had even set foot on the gravel.

She smiled and scooped him up in her arms. A rush of love made tears prick at her eyes as she saw her mum and her little boy.

"Hey mum, was he good?"

As always, he was a little angel her mother replied, "Are you good to go?"

Katie nodded and pointed to the cases neatly stacked in the boot. Three cases, three new lives. Her mother had always wondered what exactly her daughter's second job was, but ask no questions, hear no lies.

"Well, we better get going then."

Katie strapped her reason for living carefully into the car seat.

"Mummy no more working late?"

"No baby never again."

Satisfied he flopped down into his seat as the three of them began the drive to the airport.

Suddenly he frowned and said, "But mummy what do you do?"

Katie glanced at her mother and said, "I help people to solve problems."

20

Dark Desire

by Munmun Aidasani

Like most middle-class family dreams, Riya's father also dreamt of his daughter's settled life. Preet was a smart-looking guy; he was handling his family business in the Hotel industry. He took responsibility after his father's death five years back. His mother left to live her life as a monk, right after his father's death.

Riya's daddy was working in Preet's office as an accountant. Preet had seen Riya in the office before. He liked her the moment he saw her; he even sent a proposal to her parents for marriage with Riya. Within a month, they both tied the nuptial knot. Riya left her parents behind and came to a new world, new life, holding Preet's hand and having boundless dreams in her eyes. The two people being strangers were gradually trying to adapt to each other's wishes.

Since childhood, Riya had been a part of a blended family. Her father tried hard to make it a replica of the first family, but it often ended up with frustration, confusion, and disappointment between Riya and her stepmother. Riya was never able to get over the loss of her mother.

Riya's stepmother always abused her and used to cast spells to eradicate her malicious-step daughter from her life, and finally, she succeeded when Riya got married.

Riya always felt isolated and felt afraid to even look at her reflection in the mirror. Riya was overwhelmed with grief and despair. Perhaps it was her sense of loneliness coupled with agony, which drove her crazy. She made up her mind to scribble down all her unalloyed feelings in her diary, which acted as the most trusted friend of her, with whom she could share her feelings without fear of being disclosed.

She was reserved about her personal life and hardly talked to her friends, but the person who influenced and shaped her life in so many different ways with her actions and thoughtful discussions was none other than her best friend Reena. Unlikely Riya, Reena had the opportunity to decide her things on her own. Growing up with such an exceptionally strong girl, she tried to develop the enthusiasm she has. She used to fantasize about Reena's ideal life. She seemed to be consumed by the personality and normalcy in life of Reena, which many times overpowers her and directs Riya to chase her dreams.

Preet, on the other hand, always took marriage as a responsibility. Much to Riya's dismay, even after two years of being together, their marriage didn't consummate. Riya's first concern was that she felt like an outside help, or like hired help but not as a wife. Preet was the kindest, gentlest, most generous husband one could ask for, But Preet never wanted her in bed.

Riya tried to approach him, but he somehow managed to elude her as always. She left no stone unturned to impress Preet or make him drool over her, but nothing seemed to work. Preet never got a hard erection, and he didn't want to see a doctor about it. He was too busy in his business that sex-life he hardly took seriously.

Overtime, Riya found herself shutting down. It was hard for her not to have her physical needs met night after night, year after year. Years of frustration, pleading, and even rage, yielded nothing. Riya had accepted that if a man doesn't want you, you can't force him to do a thing that fascinates you. Sometimes Riya wondered how the distance between two people on a queen-sized bed could be so vast, so unbridgeable. It would have been a lot easier for Riya to walk out of the marriage if Preet was mean and nasty to her, but he never was. To the world, they were a perfect couple, holding hands in parties, events, and celebrating anniversaries.

During all these years, the writer in Riya took a back seat, somewhere along the way, while navigating through her school and college exams. After graduation, her parents decided that she needed the most important degree that is someone's wife, and started her journey from 'Miss.' to 'Mrs.' So, just to be what her parents wanted her to be, she started a new chapter in her life.

But this hobby was continued by Reena of which Riya was not aware of. Reena used to write all her experiences and feelings more personal, along with the room number.

Reena's phone beeped.

"Can we meet?"

Her heart said, "No!"

But still, she texted back, "Hotel Leelawati 9 p.m."

Mr. Patel and Reena sat across the table, inside the room no. 102.

"Would you like to have some wine?" Mr. Patel asked

"No, Mr. Patel, I am fine!" Said Reena.

"Could you please stay some more time? I will pay you extra."

"Aghh I hate the word EXTRA!" Reena mutters with aggression.

"You know my rules, Mr. Patel, I made you clear everything before any commitment," Reena said firmly.

I have another meeting right away, Mr. Patel.

She was tired of hearing the word "extra" everywhere. She was quite aware of Riya's situation of being an "extra" in an otherwise perfect family, as she was a stepdaughter, to the "extra" in Preet's life. Her existence had always revolved around this word. She was much like those freebies that come along with grocery shopping. Her self-respect was at stake. She always felt ignored and unwanted. She knew how her friend had tried to revive her relationships, but all efforts in vain.

Soon, Reena left the hotel room at her promised time and headed towards the bar of the hotel, to meet her friend Riya. Riya and Reena mostly end up meeting in bars, clubs, and pubs.

That day Preet reached the hotel for his business meet and he was shocked to look at his wife in the dance bar. He thought he would go and check with Riya, the reason behind her presence in the bar after reaching home, as that was not the right time to converse.

Reena left for home and so as Riya.

Riya reached home and was surprised to see Preet, as he came earlier than usual.

Preet inquired Riya, "Where were you Riya?"

Riya replied, "I went to meet my friend, Reena, as she organized a small party in the bar of Hotel Leelawati."

Preet was worried, as he had not seen anyone around Riya at that time. He wanted to know what Riya was hiding?

On another side, the ladies of the community gathered daily after dinner for their late evening walk. The list of gossip was endless, and so were their talks. Off late, the target of their tittle-tattle was the new occupant of the villa across the road.

They all eyed Reena as she got down from the car.

This guy frequently drops Mrs. Rai to Mrs. Sabharwal.

"Who knows where she is going? Is this the time to return?" Mrs. Sabharwal scorned.

"The rich people think as if they can do anything, and no one will question them. I pity her husband, who is such a rich man and married such a middle-class girl, busy in his business all day and night, and having no idea where his wife is staying till the mid-nights."

Everyone was looking at her garish dressing and scornful looks.

Reena walked hurriedly towards the gate; all the time aware of the spying glances on her but ignored them completely.

Mrs. Rai again muttered, "What a loose woman she is!"

Reena after entering her house, took her diary out, noted down Room-102, Mr. Hardik Patel, Hotel Leelawati, Date..., Number..., and remarked as Reena.

By doing so, she was getting immense pleasure and satisfaction, which she never experienced before.

That night, Reena mistakenly left her possession by her bedside table.

The next morning, Preet was looking for some important documents. He searched every nook and corner of the house, looked through the drawers of the bedside table, but it was nowhere to be found. Suddenly he came across the personal journal. He curiously opened that diary.

One of the oddities of reading the diary of someone he has never met or knew about that person, even the measured way in which the writer recorded the details, which was enough to bring up a distinct image of her.

It wasn't just inquisitiveness that glued Preet to this diary. It was eroticism. He wanted to find out who the writer of this journal could be? What was the mystery behind her each recording? How was that diary lying in his house? Preet's mind underwent a never-ending roller coaster ride from morning till night. His mind was subject to emotional tides. He wanted to discuss this diary with Riya but was worried about her reaction. He was all the time puzzled about who Reena was.

The other night, Reena got another beep.

"Tomorrow Hotel Mascot 9 p.m. Can we meet?" Mr. Agarwal questioned.

Reena deep in her thoughts... I don't know what honeypot the escorts or prostitutes have. No husband seems happy with his wife.

"Ok, Mr. Agarwal I will reach on time." She texted back.

Reena's policy was to never visit the same person. But you never know that life has many blindfolds, Fate and fortune are never controlled, and all plans decided by you are sometimes clean bowled.

Reena wore a clinging black dress and left home with a bold look.

She reached the reception and asked for Room 109, as mentioned by Mr. Agarwal.

Soon she headed towards the room and rang the bell. Mr. Preet Agarwal was eagerly waiting to escort Ms. Reena, in his skin-tight boxer shorts and was looking so hot.

Yes, Mr. Agarwal was none other than Preet, Riya's husband.

Preet was astonished to look at his wife this way. Riya had already suffered a lot, which triggered her personality and aspects due to childhood trauma as being an 'Extra' everywhere. Riya always wished that her mind functions like others. She screams when she is angry, cries her heart out when sad, laughs wholeheartedly, is determined to do everything as and when she feels like doing it, not bothered about the aftermath and stress. But her mind seems to be caught up in knots of the past experiences and future apprehensions. No matter how eloquently she quotes that she should live in the present, but when it comes to applying the quote in practically, she fails. An emotional scar from the past keeps rearing, its ugly head. Her past was always a reminder of the unbearable agony she went through, which takes over a toll on her present life.

Riya was overshadowed by Reena that tore every element of her life. She never let go of Reena as she wanted to attain everything in her life, which she was deprived of, and she could fulfill all her dark desires with the help of Reena. However, Riya was oblivious to the fact she was enduring all this for so long.

Riya always tried to keep her married life safe, for no reason whatsoever.

Her husband fails to understand the basics of sex and married life, which buried her emotions somewhere due to society's prejudices and taboos. It was a matter of heart and body; where comes the role of Reena. Suffocating silence regarding sex and the stigma associated with it gave birth to Reena. Reena, a fancy girl never lets Riya go to protect Riya's innocence but at the same time, she clings to her and forces her emotions and sensations to be heightened. Riya's true soul was absorbed by Reena who was not even in existence. Riya was unaware of Reena who was killing her from inside like a parasite, and this truth came out when Preet confronted Riya to her as a character Reena that consumed her darkness.

Reena was a person who goes as an escort or prostitute to satisfy her optimal lust.

But how can we call a lady whore, by keeping away all the possible reasons that tend her to become a prostitute or an escort?

It portrays that sometimes brutal and unrealistic pictures or visions of the worst-case scenarios happen. However, it is not designed to give guidance or techniques that may not be practical for everybody.

21

Faulty Hope Of Dawn

by Sumeet Doondani

One fine day I was being quite that depressed version of myself all over again, about the situations happening around me. I felt numb again as if I fell off the highest peak. I was not able to divert my mind again and I was lying at the corner of my bed again, the corner where I over thought every damn thing of my life. Suddenly I felt like a neuron rushed all over the place. It happened all over again and it felt as if I was drowning in mere blackness furthermore. I lost the purpose of my existence and my darkness was all left in me. The darkness that I buried some years ago was on its surface again. I was back to the place where it all happened, the place that swallowed me sliver by sliver. I don't know-how but in my darkness, Miley found me again. To pull me off from the end that was about to tear itself once again. To be very honest she's more of a positive and brighter side than me being into a darker and depressing side. She felt that something was wrong as I missed my lectures and wasn't there. So she attacked my room to cheer me up.

I met Miley six months ago in my sophomore year. She brought me and my happiness no matter how crappy my day was.

Hannah utters, "I am here to share the biggest secret of life with you!"

Miley's face was pale and she replied, "Oh! Now you will erupt that secret on my shoulders?"

Hannah said, "You are the one who creates vacuum space in me, which keeps me floating even when I have failed from being happy and loved anyone around me or myself to the moon and back. Rather you are the happy girl."

Miley hushed, "Yes Hannah! Because everyone should fall in love all over again. And never find reasons for that at all. No person should ever try to fill their soul with that hollow portion. Just be merrier and cherish every moment they are blessed to have."

Hannah stared at her, "Something always leaves me to feel deserted. I am filled with all my sorrows. It seems damn difficult to replenish myself with something beautiful!"

Miley replies steadily, "The reason behind this is

Even after all your achievements and attainment, you ask for more attention, appreciation, approvals, acceptance just to enlarge your identity, your fame, your ego, and this is why you remain miserable for all your life and still be in deep shit that's not even that big of a deal.

You try to find light in the world around you but when you should peek into your heart, the sun is somewhere deeply rooted in you, Hannah!"

Hannah asked her out of exception and an unnecessary void in her voice, "What do you mean, Miley?"

Miley replies calmly, "When you feel desolation in your sorrows, learn to never close your heart and mind in any kind of grief or grudges for somebody."

Hannah murmurs, "Can you please care to explain to me more."

Miley smirks and utters, "Okay! Laugh when you can, apologize when you should, let go of what you cannot change. To make it simpler, tell me if you have to choose between a blank canvas or a mere sheet filled with colours. What will you select?"

Hannah replied with ecstasy, "That blank canvas. I guess..."

Miley smiles silently and says, "Even if the canvas is blank fill it with the colours of love, joy...

Be naughty, chase adventure, enjoy pleasure, take more risks, dance a lot, crack jokes, make some mistakes legal though. Even if something or someone breaks your heart, then find a way to flirt more, do mischief, turn your perception, enjoy more, worry less, laugh till your stomach hurts, do things which seem crazy. Satisfy every element of your body just like the little bud blooming up like a fresh rose."

Hannah wonders and asks Miley, "You mean to say that the light resides inside me, and I can madly seek it outside in the world too? That happiness and that light."

Miley with happiness, "Yes! I am always here by your side.

You are perfect and never forget that.

A state full of love, joy, happiness, bliss..."

And that's where Hannah and Miley's bond became stronger than before, that too for a lifetime and their lives continued to be in this state of harmony forever. Fingers crossed.

Hannah was living in her abandoned house in the same room where her parents were murdered in cold blood. Where the sheets and floor still had stains of her parent's blood, the room that she is scared to clean up. And the heart that still beats faster every time she looked through that cracked window into her garden where she buried her parents. That small happy family was all she had, the togetherness. She lived in a remote area somewhere on the outskirts of New Orleans where no case could ever be solved. The place which was somewhat miles away from Hannah's school too. She dropped out of school last year. Since her parents died, she never replied to the calls of her friends, professors not even the headmaster. She vanished in thin air, almost six months ago. The calls got fewer and then just stopped. Everyone forgot about the existence of a girl named Hannah. The garden that was once filled with roses and daisies was now just barren land. The area where she lived her life to the fullest and adored all the phases of her life from crawling, cycling down the road, till the most tragic moment of her life, a mysterious murder of her parents. Her life started there and now it's just filled with some sorrows unknown. That is drowning her in the same place all over again. The place of mere blackness that is just like the black hole.

In the end, Miley and Hannah were still at the corner of the bed in front of the half shattered mirror and said the same words together.

"Umm... Where to start, the world full of personalities or a person full of personalities. The emotion of feels or the feel of emotions. The void and its darkness or the darkness of the void.

That is moving towards the end, or maybe it's the start of an end. Life goes around the world. At times the words and phrases can't be disclosed who it might be. Maybe it's well said that some secrets are better to be kept hidden."

Hannah kept gazing at that half-shattered mirror. To find something, but maybe the half-shattered mirror was after all barren too just like the garden. Miley vanished in thin air just like Hannah did six months ago.

22

Me And Myself

by Sumeet Doondani

Umm...from whom to start with... A girl with the sweetest smile or vengeance rage... A woman with a kind heart or bewitching thoughts... Or A lady with jolly nature or a depressed soul! In a great dilemma regarding how many people I am talking about? And in no time such a question will arise in your mind, right...? So much suspense; well it's for me too. And to divulge this mystery you must roll through the phases of Anaya's life once, which looks a lot like a tragedy now...! When you met her on the street, chances are you would never know. Her core is an intelligent, calm, and very straightforward woman but under the surface, you don't know what is triggering her and why?

Anaya is fragmented into pieces of herself! Her mind and heart are like a shattered mirror into dozens of pieces. The person in this situation uses the fight, flight, or freeze analogy. In a stressful situation, those are typically the options one can take. But she is being abused too often, so she can't fight or run. The memories of her past trauma that froze into her mind, and went into shock, she recalls while huddling on the hospital bed and weeping for her bewitching acts. The moments she's spending there became solitude for her where she's looking back on her past and started reciting her deeds in her mind.

"I was a little girl who stood in the corner and didn't speak and didn't raise my hand. The one who didn't speak, who was never allowed to speak, but guess what, I have a voice."

Anaya was born in a poor family and had an impoverished background. Her father Vipul was labeled as an accused primarily indulged in 'Heroine.' He lobs his every frustration upon his wife Simar. He's involved in child trafficking, extortion, money laundering, sexual and drug-abusing, exploitations, and procuring minors. These incidents started happening more frequently than ever. The torment on Simar and Anaya by Vipul was increasing more now. Vipul was becoming insensible towards his family. And one fine day he lost his senses and became the culprit of the family... The time when Simar went out to bring food grains for her family, Vipul tried to sell his 5 years daughter to one mobster who was linked to the mafia, to make up for the lost money on alcohol and cigarettes, while Anaya was sleeping in her bed. He kidnapped and abducted her into a basket with rage as she was thin and had sluggish growth and went to the mafia's door without a nuisance, over drugged and filthier. Eventually, Anaya was emancipated from this imprisonment incident of her life. This incident tore Anaya and her mother. So Simar decided to run out with her daughter from this devil's house. And they succeed in their mission. They succeed to move out of this hell. Simar took her daughter to the railway station of their village and they departed for Delhi. Anaya and Simar moved to a new city... It took 6 years for Simar and Anaya to settle themselves in a new place. A decade passed and Anaya became a teacher and started teaching in one of the famous schools in Delhi. She started evolving with time. Also, she followed her passion for self-love. She groomed herself as an artist. Her paintings make her feel alive and keep her sane. Her paintings became popular not only in her hometown but also in other cities as well.

She says, "Paintings are the Silent Poetry which Speaks. My Paintings are my Voice."

But the souvenir of her past where she only felt misdeed, villainy, torture... And all these become a part of her remembrance. Deep inside, all alone she was still struggling with her past.

On one of these days, Simar and Anaya went to the mall. They met Mohit there. The first meeting with Mohit gave her a different sense of feeling like reminiscing and mesmerizing. And this time she felt like it was love! Perhaps love at first sight! And all she started believing in miracles, magic, amazeballs! She felt out of this world! It's like she was blossoming like a baby flower. Her blood rushed into her veins as if it got the wings of a butterfly! They exchanged their numbers. And in less time, they begin their love story. She started feeling safe with Mohit after all he was the first guy with whom she was cherishing, sharing, and conveying all about her. She felt like home with him, as her own family members. Her father never cared about anything or anyone, and little affections from Mohit attract Anaya towards him. However, Mohit was a womanizer and Anaya was entirely unaware of this fact. Mohit does not want to be in a relationship with Anaya except for one nightstand. So, to quench the thirst of his lust, he started spending a lot of time with Anaya. When they both are together, Mohit secretly starts giving her drugs.

Here Anaya now started getting strange gifts like a dead flower, voodoo doll, Cat-O-Nine Tails, zombie mugs, spooky box. As she gets more romantic with Mohit, gifts get more extreme.

Out of much ignition, he asked her for one night of the engagement. But Anaya denied. So now he started losing his temper. The urge to fill his lust was overloading, and this leads him to abuse Anaya sexually. Also, he exhorted her that if she won't set up a physical relationship with him, he will kill her mother. She broke up with Mohit. In the present circumstances, along with Anaya, Mohit is also getting threat calls. The one phone call left Mohit in a great bizarre state. The person asked him to meet in the evening at Anaya's house. Mohit felt something peculiar and got very much tensed and very scared because it's been a couple of weeks since they broke up, and who is calling him and asking to meet at Anaya's place. On the other side, Simar was unaware of their breakup and kept dreaming about them.

Under the influence of stress and all these circumstances, Anaya's mind started evoking the incidence of past harassment done by her father and recent demands of her mother, her mind started spinning. She is not understanding what to do further? She was then found to be violent even to the people who were close to her.

This could range from:-

4 Night terrors

3 Venomous Thoughts

2 Homicidal

1 Suicidal Attempts.

And her room was filled with darkness. The floor there seems like a route from the highway to hell. All the things in the room are scattered everywhere. On the spur of the movement, the night lamp started blinking. Out of the blue, the shadow becomes visible by the reflection of the moonlight and before you can say a knife, the footsteps of a lady become audible. She is coming into the room. The door opened up and shut with a bangarang noise. And she dragged her aggressively. She pulled the knife from the pocket of her jacket and cut the lady's neck off. Then she placed the body in the bathtub and left the tap open. And The murderer night went off. In the morning when Anaya woke up and started looking at her mother in the house, as of her daily routine. Engrossing here and there she reached up to the washroom, the scene made her numb. She can't believe what her eyes were watching. She was screaming and gasping for breath. She saw the dead body of her mother Simar. The bathtub was filled with water, it seemed like a bloodbath, a reign of terror. She thought this was done by Mohit, and in no time She informed the police and told them about the incident. She also hired a detective. As the police arrived, Anaya explained to them about the strange gifts, and sexual harassment by Mohit followed by their breakup. The police and detectives took Mohit in remand and preceded the investigation with him. Eventually, Mohit was shocked too, when he came to know about Simar's death because he was not guilty of her death. He only gave a fake warning to Anaya. But he didn't intend to do so. Then who did this? Who took Simar's life? Who opened the door to death for Simar and why? The cessation of Simar was a turning point in Anaya's life.

The police and detectives approach the scene. They initiated preliminary survey-including supervision on open windows, damaged doors, ladders, and the like. Evaluating the physical evidence was too followed. As the investigation goes on, police and detectives find traces of blood in other areas of the room and there were visible footprints in blood as well. One camera footage of Anaya's house was seen by the investigating team. And through video clips and traces of footprints in blood, it came to know that it was done by Simar's daughter, Anaya. And as police came to arrest Anaya in the charge of her mother's death, she snatched the rifle from the pocket of the jacket of the constable and tried to shoot herself. She got injured in harming herself and the authorities took her to the hospital. As soon as She regains her senses, she finds herself surrounded by the police team. But this time, it's not Anaya in front of them. The human was not Anaya, she was the murderer.

"I am her protector and she is my caretaker. I am her supporter and she is my defender. I am here to be with her. And I am here to take revenge for her suffering. We are neither the same nor different. We are two in one being. I am Ayesha and she is Anaya." She said and her eyes were filled with rage.

Ayesha is her other personality. Anaya splinted into a dual personality because of the trauma she faced in her childhood by her father and sexual harassment by her boyfriend Mohit. To relieve the pain and sufferings of both incidents, she took the support of herself, of her own.

23

Wilted Rose

by Vaishali Chandorkar Chitale

Harsh looked at his wife, confused. She was on the phone with Rohini, her sister-in-law (brother's wife) berating her about something. Her voice was shrill and strident. This was not the Preeti he knew. His Preeti was soft-spoken, gentle, and kind. What had got into her, he wondered? This was the first time he had seen her this angry.

They had been married for two years now. When they first met, Harsh had been captivated by Preeti's charm and winsome nature. When they say opposites attract, they surely know what they are talking about. He had liked her the moment he saw her. He had gone to Preeti's Home with his parents, to 'see' her and liked her within a second. He had found her not just beautiful, which she was; but also delightful. His reserved nature and the habit of weighing his words before speaking was in total contrast to her spontaneity which he took to immediately. His family tended to have a serious outlook, what with his father being a Judge in Sessions Court and the atmosphere at home was always rather somber, as befitting a senior judge's home. Preeti brought a whiff of fresh air in their house and her laughter brought a smile to his face every time he heard it.

They stayed with his parents, initially. As a fresh law graduate, he didn't earn enough to support both of them. His parents lived in a sprawling bungalow in the heart of the city and there was enough room for all of them without getting into each other's hair. It was a perfect arrangement, as far as he was concerned.

His mother and younger sister got along with Preeti merrily. His father, however, was a different story. A strict disciplinarian and a stickler for routine, he was baffled by her casual attitude. But she soon won him over too by her beguiling presence.

Things went smoothly at first. He was pleased to have his soul mate, life looked bright and rosy. Coming home to that smiling face every day, made him forget his hard day at work. She had in her quiet unassuming way taken the responsibility of running the house. His mother couldn't stop singing her praises and his father had taken to smiling benignly at her pottering about the house. He often found his sister stuck with Preeti exchanging girly gossip. They soon became close confidants. His parents were even talking now of retiring, going to their village, and leading a quiet life, quite assured that their son was in good hands.

But today seeing his wife lashing out at her sister-in-law got him back to the present sharply. His affable wife had turned into something unrecognizable. He managed to prise the phone away from her and quieted her down. She glared at him angrily. He made her sit on the sofa to calm her down and regain composure. He was unfamiliar that he had no words to describe what he had just seen.

The next day was even more surprising. When he attempted to ask Preeti about the incident, she had no recollection of the same. She laughed at him for even thinking that she could have shouted at Rohini. Perturbed, he let it past, not wanting to disturb the peace of the house. He desperately wanted to believe that it was a one-off occurrence. On the looks of it, everything seemed as normal as day and night, but Preeti had changed imperceptibly.

But more was in store. Once he came home to see Preeti cowering in the corner of their room. When he repeatedly asked, Preeti confessed that his father had locked her in the room this afternoon because he was disturbed by her music. She complained that his father was critical of everything she said or did, and was given to bouts of anger if things didn't go as he wanted or asked for. A genuine small mistake or an oversight offended him no end. He often punished her like a schoolgirl. She was terrified of him and desperately wanted a home of her own. This was so absurd a charge, that he was at his wits' end to understand what was happening.

It was as if there were two Preetis; one a docile, charming wife who went about minding her own business, and the other a scheming, vindictive person whom he could not relate to. Her violent outbursts came in too suddenly and without any warning. It became an almost everyday occurrence. There was no saying which Preeti would greet him when he came home. His parents and sister were baffled by the situation and looked at him for an answer. His father even asked him worriedly whether everything was fine between them and were there any marital issues (as in physical relations) between them.

He found it strange, he thought, when Preeti, despite her excellent credentials and education, was happy being a homemaker. She never had aspirations to work or do a job. It was fine by him; he was making enough for them to live lavishly and afford an occasional holiday now. But her decision had surprised him, as she knew that her mother, though a homemaker, had assisted her husband in his construction business, with maintaining accounts, managing the inflow and expenditure; in fact, even going on the site to supervise, when needed. So, it was rather surprising that his wife, who he thought would have wanted to follow in her mother's footsteps, decided to do just the opposite and became a stay-at-home-wife.

When he urged her again to rethink her decision to work, he was taken aback by her answer. She insisted that he wanted her to sit at home and look after the family. No doubt, Preeti kept an immaculate house, managed the sundry family helps, had their meals served on time, looked into their investments and any other pesky detail that needed to be done while running the household, But now she had no recollection of the fact that he had on innumerable occasions told her to live her own life, besides just looking after them and running the house.

Preeti yearned to be a mother. She loved children and was looking forward to having one of her own. He thought, maybe this could be the solution to their problem. Motherhood will keep her busy and her violent mood swings (as he saw them) will cease. With that in mind, he approached her to talk about starting their own family. But to his massive shock, she vehemently opposed the idea and insisted that she was not ready to be a mother as yet. Still reeling by her reaction, he noticed for the first time, a slightly varied inflection in her voice. It was shrill, in a high pitch, somewhat like a child. He realized that she talked in this voice whenever she was not the Preeti he knew.

He was finding it difficult to reconcile the two Preeti's that he now saw almost on a daily basis. Anything triggered a shift in her personality. His coming late from office, could one day make her fly in a violent rage and on another day smile benignly and offer him a cup of tea. This see-sawing Preeti was difficult to fathom.

He didn't understand the gravity of the situation until one day, when he received a phone call from his sister, while at work. His wife was threatening to slit her wrists because of some trivial difference of opinion with his father. She was in an uncontrollable rage and difficult to control. He was aghast that she could think of taking such a drastic step over something which could have been easily resolved. This Preeti was not the person he had married!

Alarmed by the worsening condition of his wife's mental condition and seeing his parent's bewilderment, he decided to consult a psychologist. He was astounded to hear the word 'split personality' associated with his wife. The doctor informed in short, that this Dissociative Identity Disorder (DID) is usually a reaction to trauma as a way to help a person avoid bad memories. He was further horrified to know that one cannot say which was the real Preeti. The affable person they all generally knew or the shrill, aggressive Preeti that she sometimes became. This split in personality was mainly caused because of some abuse faced by the patients in their childhood, which could be sexual or emotional.

To date, Preeti had not been forthright about her family and past. She never talked about her childhood, had no memories to share which though he had found strange, he had glossed over it, as he had more than enough for both of them. Whenever he had tried to delve into her childhood, wanting to know her as a baby or even the teenage self, she would always change the topic. He reflected, possibly, this was where the seeds of Preeti's growing disorder if one can call it that, were sown. She refused to speak about her family and her relations. There was a joint family, with Preeti's uncle's (father's elder brother) family, living in the same compound. Now he wanted to know more, search into her past for clues.

The therapist had advised him to sit with his wife, and gently encourage her to talk about her past. Be a confidant and not judge anything that she shares. She needs to be handled with love and kindness before it is too late.

One evening, seeing his wife in a mellow mood, he decided to seize the moment. Tenderly taking her near, he probed her about her childhood. Caught in a vulnerable mood his wife for once, opened up about her past. Her outpourings came out in a rush. It was as if a dam had broken and she could not stop. He was appalled to know that she had undergone sexual abuse at the hands of their neighbour, who was a very good friend of her uncle's. Her grandfather and his father had known each other since childhood. Her father and his brother had grown up with the neighbour and they considered him family. He used to come home in the afternoons when her parents were out on work and he forced himself on her. It used to hurt down there. She was too young to understand and could not tell anyone what she was going through. Her parents left her to her uncle's place in the afternoons and he used to find her there too. Ostensibly wanting to cuddle her, he used to touch her at inappropriate places done so cunningly that her aunt never noticed. She lived in fear and dreaded his appearance at their home. She had withdrawn into herself, but no one saw anything amiss as she was anyways a quiet child.

This state of affairs continued till God took pity on her and her tormentor was transferred to a different city on promotion, by his company. But the scars of those days remained and her fear of those days made her anxious and sometimes confused about her present life.

He desperately wanted his Preeti back from whatever demons she was fighting within herself and knew he would do whatever it takes to accomplish that. The girl whom he had fallen in love with is lost somewhere in the maze of her mind and she needed his empathy and support to overcome that. He was prepared to move mountains if need be to see a happy carefree Preeti once again. He knew it was not an impossible dream, and with his support and love, and therapy her insecurities and fear could be laid to rest to a large extent. He was sure, with his tender love and care, his wilted rose would bloom again.

24

Life Fragmented

by Vaishali Chandorkar Chitale

The Ambulance rushed through the crowded streets, blaring its siren, and the beacon light flashing furiously. The evening rush hour traffic added to its woes. The van towered over the sea of blinking red lights with no way out. The driver, an expert at navigating his vehicle out of chaos, was trying his best to inch forward by turning the steering in all directions and honking desperately for the cars in the front to let them pass.

Inside the van, the patient, twenty-five years old, Radhika was being administered IVS fluids by the paramedics, to keep her conscious. To stop her bleeding, they had tied a tourniquet around her wrists and covered her with blankets for her to overcome her shock. Her mother Uma sitting beside them couldn't stop crying. She closed her eyes to pray for Radhika. Her husband and son were following the ambulance in their car. She could see their worried faces through the glass and knew they too were praying for Radhika's life.

On reaching the hospital, the paramedics handed Radhika to the hospital staff who rushed her to the Emergency for treatment. Uma sat down wearily on a bench and let her son and husband take over. What had made Radhika take her life? Why had she slit her wrists? What had compelled her to take this drastic step? all these questions were swirling in Uma's head.

The day had dawned as usual. Uma got up early, like every other day to make their breakfast, which on weekdays was basic eggs and fruit, followed by instant coffee for all. Shirish and she worked long hours; she was an HR head in a computer software company and Shirish in his architectural firm. Aditya was studying to be an architect and Radhika was employed in a PR office.

The morning was like all the mornings but had gone in a flurry of activity, with all of them getting ready for the day and leaving within half an hour of each other with their tiffins in their bags. She had not noticed anything unusual about Radhika that day. Yes, to be sure Radhika was in a fragile bend of mind but Uma had an unobtrusive eye on her always.

For the last couple of months, Uma had noticed a change in Radhika. Though the accident had occurred almost a year back, it had seemed that Radhika had got over it and was on the mend. Radhika had been engaged to her childhood sweetheart Aman for a year, before the accident. They were planning to get married after saving some money, as they wanted to host their wedding. They were quite firm that they wanted a small intimate affair with only the close family and friends for the function. Both the set of parents had given in good-naturedly and the happy occasion was being looked forward to.

But the tragedy had struck most unexpectedly and thrown their life askew. Radhika and Aman had gone to Lonavala with their friends for some weekend fun and a sort of the last fling as singles before they tied the knot. It had been Aman's idea and Radhika was all for it as they had the same set of friends. They were ten of them and were about to go together in two hired cabs. But the last-minute work at Aman's office had them following later in their car.

It was on their way back that the ghastly accident had occurred. A speeding truck had dashed into Aman's car from behind with so much force that the car had turned turtle and struck the road divider on the driver's side. Aman was killed on the spot and Radhika had suffered serious injuries to her spine and head. They had been informed by their friends who were following them and had rushed to the hospital. After some days, Radhika, barely conscious, had been shifted to a hospital in Mumbai, for further treatment.

But it had been a long road to recovery. Radhika had been operated on twice for her spinal cord injury and had been in the ICU for almost a month. Nobody had dared to tell her about Aman in those initial days. The doctors had warned them that she will need tender and patient care for her to come out of this trauma and had advised them to take each day as it comes. When her questions could no longer be ignored, they had to tell her about Aman. She had taken the news calmly which had surprised everyone at that time, but unfortunately, no one gave it further thought.

After a two month stay in the hospital, Radhika had been discharged and came home, physically recovering but broken inside. It was heart-wrenching to see her lying listlessly on the bed, shutting out the world. She had to be coaxed into eating and the family rallied around by cooking her favourite dishes so that she could gain her strength back earliest.

Being young and resilient, Radhika soon got on her feet. To Uma's dismay, her young effervescent daughter had changed into a quiet one, speaking only when spoken to and wanting only to be by herself. She and Shirish had thought that with time, she would bounce back and things would come back to normal. How wrong and short-sighted they had been!

Uma started noticing little things at first. One day, she heard Radhika talking to her friend on the phone and making plans for going out the next day. She was however surprised at the slightly shrill babyish tone of her voice. Also, the fact that she wanted to go to a movie about an actor like she didn't like it at all. Not giving it a second thought, she was happy that Radhika was getting back to her old self. So, she was intrigued when she saw Radhika at home and was taken aback when Radhika denied having any plans of going out with friends. She had no recollection of the previous day's conversation.

Radhika had always been an avid reader and occasionally penned some poems also. Post-accident, Uma to her utter amazement, saw Radhika making beautiful watercolour landscapes, blending and shading like a seasoned artist. Radhika hummed to herself while painting and her face reflected happiness. Uma was relieved that Radhika had picked up a hobby. So, her bewilderment was complete when Radhika asked her one afternoon about the paintings and wanted to know who had painted them. A small little seed of niggling worry settled in her mind.

Radhika had changed imperceptibly. Sometimes her usual self, reading and helping her in the kitchen, sometimes so distant and stranger like; her gaze so unrecognizing that Uma felt a sliver of fear. She had severe mood changes within a day. Happy and painting in the mornings, she would suddenly retreat in her world and mope around the house. By the evening, she would be singing in a different voice, songs which they had never heard her sing before. These mood swings, as they saw it, were as baffling as fish flying in the air.

Radhika had also taken to throwing violent tantrums. She would lose her temper on something as trivial as the food not to her liking or breakfast not ready on time. She would stalk off in anger, without taking her lunch and would not answer Uma's calls. Her quiet phase was even more worrisome. It was as if she was being shrouded by a heavy mist, which none could penetrate. Uma feared that Radhika would harm herself when in this mood and hovered around her, protectively.

The accident had taken a toll not only on Radhika but even on her family. They never knew which Radhika they would see in front of them, at any given time. All three of them had taken to treading carefully around her lest her violent bouts triggered off. But the most disturbing aspect was that Radhika had no recollection of her vicious angry outbursts after she had calmed down. She would give them disbelieving looks and be horrified that she could be accused of being aggressive.

Though Radhika had re-joined her office, she had no recollection of the accident and Aman's death. Her colleagues also rallied around and avoided talking about Aman and that fateful day. She never asked about him. Initially, Uma and Shirish thought that once the shock wears off, she would be curious to know the details. But that never happened. She took to her routine of pre-accident days and they had let the sleeping dogs lie.

Which had turned out to be their biggest mistake, Uma mused now. They should have seen the warning signs, especially when she had once caught Radhika with a bottle of sleeping pills and had been fobbed off with some lame excuse of having trouble falling to sleep and so kept them, just in case. Why had she not questioned her motives then? When had Radhika decided to end her life? Or was it just a cry for help?

Shirish and Aditya joined her on the bench, haggard and tired. The doctors were attending to her, though she had lost a lot of blood, she would survive. Uma sent heartfelt thanks of gratitude to God and vowed to take care of Radhika, whatever it takes.

The doctor soon summoned them to his cabin. They were told that the police will have to be informed as it was an attempted suicide case. On hearing her history and the puzzling behaviour which they described, the doctor informed them that in most probability she was suffering from DID (Dissociative Identity Disorder) a condition brought about by extreme trauma suffered by the patient. Radhika losing Aman and the horrific accident had left her in a shock, which she had dealt with by detaching herself from the memories. She had regressed in the time before the accident but, in layman's language, the trauma had triggered off some stress-related reactions in her brain and she escaped into different persons at different times.

He advised them to show Radhika to a therapist who would suggest a line of treatment for Radhika to recover her 'memories' and retrieve her past. She may have to be referred to a hypnotist also. It was a long arduous journey ahead, he warned them, but with the treatment, she had a chance of living a normal life. Uma and Shirish exchanged a relieved look, now at least they knew the cause of Radhika's behavioural change. They had finally got a direction and were ready to face any hurdle to get their daughter back.

As they walked towards Radhika's room, Uma felt a spring in her step. Striding through the corridor she saw a window slightly open and the early morning sun rays peeping in like a silver lining as if to say that tomorrow is another day and will bring forth joy and happy tidings.

25

What Happens, Happens For A Reason? (Part I)

by Vishakha Naware

It is a bright and sunny morning, as it is the beginning of summer in New York, Central Park is already abuzz with joggers, casual walkers, and picnickers. I have packed our picnic basket with Melissa's favourite salmon and peanut butter sandwiches, a very odd combination, but she just loves it! In the basket, there are also Simon's favorite caprese sandwiches made using mozzarella and the juicy seasonal tomatoes from the farmer's market. Simon has recently turned vegetarian and we are always looking for interesting vegetarian recipes for him.

As we find a comfortable spot in the East Green, very popular with families with small children, we lay our blanket and sit down for a moment before Melissa could head for the swings. We have chosen this spot because later we had plans to visit the Central Park Zoo which is right across the street and Mel loves to watch the sea lions and penguins there. Saturdays are usually spent in the park with a visit to the zoo.

Simon and I cherish these moments that we spend with Mel as we are very busy during the week.

I look at Simon, fondly, as he takes Mel to the swings. They cackle and giggle and he tries to catch her when she runs away. It is so good watching them together- the man that I love so much and the daughter who has completed our lives. My memories take me back to the fateful day when Simon and I met. Simon, oh, my Simon- he is just under six feet tall, his eyes brown like hazel, glistening when the sunbeam reaches them. His dark toffee-coloured hair shines in the sun and the curls flow unruly with the wind. I remember his cheerful smile on his glowing face when I opened up my eyes in the hospital.

I met Simon in the Lenox Hill Hospital on 77th Street. Our first meeting was rather unusual and very dramatic. I was being carried away to the Emergency Room as somehow, I was caught in between a gang war and was shot in the process. I was at the wrong time in the wrong place. Strike that, I was at my usual walking spot in Central Park one evening. It was my favourite spot as not many people would prefer to come here (now I know the reason why!) and I would like to be left alone with my thoughts sometimes, especially as I had just broken up with my long-time boyfriend, James.

James had warned me about my walking spot and as a vengeful decision after our beak-up, I decided to visit it more often! He had no business warning me now that he had broken up with me.

On that evening, I became aware of two shady-looking guys, who came near me, near the bench where I usually rested after a brisk walk. They came out, not towards me, but near me. So, initially, I ignored them, got up, and kept walking, thinking to myself that I need to get the hell out of there as soon as possible. Also, cursing myself for not listening to James.

I had seen that they were looking straight at each other in fury and one of them had a tattoo on his right arm, it was a tattoo of letters written in a skull, letters AC and realization dawned upon me that an infamous drug-dealing gang had the same initials. So, I just wanted to get the hell out of there. I was walking at a very rapid pace and just after a few moments, there was a piercing sound in my head. I felt like the world was collapsing around me. Everything was a blur and I could hardly feel anything, sense anything. My mouth was dry and after a few moments, it was mere darkness! Then a few moments later, I managed to regain some consciousness and the last thing that I could remember was me being carried from the ambulance to the hospital. I had opened my eyes for a few minutes and there were people around me rushing me into the ER, telling me to focus on staying awake, but I failed to do so. Amongst the many people around me, carrying me to the ER, I especially noticed a face, a man in scrubs, looking all worried at me. His face just made an imprint on me, even in that state of mental delirium. I could feel something for him. The next moment, darkness befell me.

Later I learned that luckily for me, the gunshot wound had caused a mild traumatic brain injury and surgery could help me. The operation had taken a couple of hours and I regained consciousness the next day. In the wee hours of the morning, I opened my eyes and there he was looking at me with that beautiful smile of his.

"How are you feeling?" He asked me, his gaze fixed on me.

"I don't remember what happened exactly. How did I land here?" I asked, my speech was slurred.

"You are on a lot of medication right now and your wound needs at least two weeks to heal. You are lucky that the bullet just grazed at your skull and didn't penetrate it. So, just a few weeks of rest and you'll be as healthy as ever!" He smiled at me.

A realization came over me that the piercing sound that I had heard was of the gunshot and the bullet had grazed me and I had fallen unconscious. Later I learned that two joggers also heard the sound and when they arrived at the scene, the gang members already fled, and there I was, lying unconscious and they quickly had called 911 for help.

I met Simon every day now as he was my appointed nurse and he would come twice or thrice a day to change my dressing or just to check up on me. He was a handsome guy with an average height and built, and when he smiled, he just lit up the room, at least for me. It was love at second sight for me, probably because I was almost unconscious when I saw him first. Yes, I remembered him being one of the team members carrying me to the ER.

We immediately bonded over our love for classic films and Mexican cuisine. I told him about the lip-smacking tamales that my abuela made when I was a child and he told me about the chilaquiles that his mama made, as she is of Mexican origin. Just two days of knowing each other and I knew that he had feelings for me too. But we had to wait to ask each other out as I was a patient there. On my last day in the hospital, he came to me and said, "Isabel, I know we have something here, but as per hospital policy, I cannot share my number with you or ask for your number. So here is my friend's number, Peter. Just call him after you're completely recovered and he will give you my number."

I smiled and was also very surprised at his slyness. "Of course," I replied.

"Also, it is very common to have nightmares or to get anxious for your safety. These are very common PTSD symptoms. So please take care of yourself and be sure you stay with someone close to you, so that you feel better," he said with a hint of worry in his eyes.

"My mother has already flown from Chicago and will be staying with me for a few weeks. My sister will also be joining us in a couple of days. So, don't you worry," I replied, trying to console him.

I couldn't believe that just in a week, that too under heavy medication and other procedures, I found love. I never had much luck when it came to love and relationships, but here, in these dire conditions, I had somehow managed to find that glimmer of hope, of new love.

I was discharged in a few days and with huge sorrow, I left the hospital. I hoped to feel better soon, I hoped that I met him again, I hoped that something turned out for us, a meaningful and beautiful relationship. This hope made me strong and I decided to work on bettering myself.

Exactly after 40 days, when things were better for me and I had also joined back at the architecture firm in the East Village that I worked for, I called Peter and asked him for Simon's number. It seemed so old school and there was just so much thrill! Finally, I will be able to hear his rustic voice again.

"Hello! How have you been? Better now?" He chirped into the phone when I called him. He had almost instantaneously recognized my voice and was over the moon that I had called him. I was very happy too and we made plans to meet on the following Friday night at the cozy Italian place, just three blocks from my place. We dined and laughed and shared our history on the first date. We kept on meeting in the days to come and after three months he had moved in with me in my three-room apartment. We lived together for a year and then we just knew that we were meant to be together and got married that July. Our families got along really well and everything was like it was just out of a dream! Simply too perfect!

After a couple of years, we had Melissa and our little family felt so complete. We were blessed with support from our families and of our nanny, Paula, hence we both could continue working full time.

Melissa is now eight years old and our family is as pretty as a picture. Today, on our eleventh wedding anniversary, we couldn't have found a better way to celebrate than to just be with each other with our picnic basket, eating sandwiches, and visiting the zoo. These small moments make life worth so much more.

As we walk together, ready to go to the zoo, I hear that piercing sound again. I feel the world collapsing around me, my mouth drying and I lose all the senses! I faintly hear people crying and shouting near me and amongst them is a cry from a little girl, my little girl, my Mel. My Mel is bawling inconsolable sobs. What is happening? Mel, where are you going… Where am I going? Mel! Simon! Can you hear me? Complete darkness befalls me!

26

What Happens, Happens For A Reason? (Part II)

by Vishakha Naware

A beeping sound wakes me up from what seems to be the deepest slumber that I have ever had. I feel groggy, hazed, and tired! I feel like I haven't been up for a while, haven't eaten anything properly, or haven't even showered in a long time! I feel ill and dirty, and diseasy, if that's even a word. Parched and ravenous, I look around me. I want something, I'm craving something sweet, like doughnuts sprinkled with sugar or cinnamon rolls, umm, cinnamon rolls, like the one's Mel, Simon, and I would have in the patisserie near our condo.

A few moments have passed now and there I see him, my Simon, looking at me. I looked at him and shut my eyes. There's just something wrong. Am I alright? Am I seeing things alright? There's something different about him. He is not so happy seeing that I, yet again, have survived a gunshot wound. He seems indifferent. Sadness wraps its arms against me. Why is he behaving like that? Did he forget me? Who was in the accident? A thousand questions just pop into my head and I feel sick.

Another striking thing that I notice is that he looks very young like he is a decade younger. Simon is 38 years old and when we met, he was 25 and I'm looking at him now and he looks 25! I just can't believe it! I think it is all due to the pain medication that I am on, so I just don't say anything. I think that maybe Simon is too overwhelmed to talk to me or say anything to me! I also want to know how Mel is, she must be so distraught and so scared after witnessing something like this. I try to open my mouth, but the sound just won't leave my tongue! I can't even move my hands or even my fingers. So, I just rest for the next few hours.

It is evening now and Simon is back in my room looking at my chart. The first thought that enters my mind is, "Why is he looking at my chart? Why is he behaving like a newbie nurse like he used to be at the beginning of his career?" I sense that something is wrong, something is wrong. I finally find some energy and say, "Simon, how is Mel? You haven't spoken a word to me after I woke up! What's happening? Tell me!" It comes out like a squeak rather than just questions. He stares at me for a very long moment, which, to me, seems like an eternity. Finally, he says, "I'm sorry, my name is Andrew, not Simon. I think you have mistaken me for someone else. And I don't know who Mel is. Is she your sister? Because there is this one young lady who comes to visit you regularly."

I freeze for a moment; I do not know what's happening.

"My sister's name is Kate and you know that. And you are Simon. What is happening? Can you explain it to me?" I shout at him.

He looks concerned now and says, "I'll be back in a minute. Please rest and do not try to get up."

After a few minutes, he comes back with a woman, tall and slim with blond hair. He introduces her as Dr. Kathy Miller. "Hello, how are you doing?" She asks me with an assuring smile.

"I... I don't know. This is my husband, Simon, and we have a daughter, Melissa, and he seems to have forgotten it all. He seems to have somehow become a decade younger. I... I don't know what's happening, I just can't understand!" I say as tears finally make a way out of my eyes.

Dr. Miller looks at me kindly, and says, "Miss Hernandez, please do not strain yourself so much. Take good rest today and we will talk tomorrow, I promise. You will get all your answers tomorrow."

She leaves the room with Simon or Andrew and I don't see Simon/Andrew for the rest of the day. Instead of him, they sent another nurse, an old but kind woman named Elisa. She takes good care of me and talks to me about my mother and sister as if she knows them for a long time now. She even seems to know about my nephew, Reid. The only thing that baffles me is that she speaks as if Reid is still aged seven, but last I checked; he was already in undergrad. Weird thoughts hover in my mind and I try to make sense of the events unfolding around me, but I'm just too tired so I slip into sleep.

The next day, my mom came along with my sister Kate and they were so happy to see me. We all had tears of joy and we just hugged each other for a long time. Then, they say that they need to leave as Dr. Miller needs to have a chat with me. It seems like they are hiding something. Not once do they mention anything about Mel and since yesterday Simon/Andrew is also not to be seen. Dr. Miller walks in after a few minutes and asks me how I am doing.

She looks at me and says firmly, "I know some of the incidents that have happened since yesterday has puzzled you. Can you please tell me how you met Simon and what happened after that till up to this moment?"

I find it all a little weird and yet I narrate to her everything that there is to know about Simon and me.

"Alright. Ms. Hernandez," she says and I correct her by saying, "I'm Mrs. Rubens. Mrs. Simon Rubens."

"No, you are Ms. Hernandez," she says firmly, looking at me, into my eyes that are clouded with tears. "You were admitted to our hospital because you suffered from a severe traumatic brain injury from a gunshot wound."

"Yes... But that was years ago," I interrupted her.

"Allow me to finish, please," she requests me and I let her continue. "Your wounds were so severe that we had to put you under a medically induced coma for a few weeks. You are here for almost six weeks now. The nurse that attended you yesterday, his name is Andrew Richards and he has been working with us for a year now. I believe you had a very lucid dream about him and having a family with him when you were in a comatose state. Andrew was one of the team members who brought you to the hospital from the ambulance and you were awake for a few minutes before you lost consciousness and you may have seen him in that brief moment. His image may have stuck with you and you may have had a very lucid dream of him- falling in love, having a family, everything. Lucid dreams are not very common in patients of medically induced coma, but we have reports of patients having them. I am sorry, but Ms. Hernandez, you had a breakup just a month before you got shot and somehow all those feelings- of finding new love- may have intertwined and led to these dreams. I know that it will be very difficult to accept this reality. But we will get through it together with regular therapy sessions and medication," She smiled kindly. "I will leave you alone for a few moments and then have your family join you," she said while leaving.

"Please tell them to visit me tomorrow. I need some time to process this," I requested her and she nodded in agreement. It was as if my whole world had crumbled into a million pieces. I couldn't believe that all of this- my picture-perfect family, the love of my life- it was all a dream! A dream that felt like reality, a lucid dream. I am good at processing grief and some say that I'm the most practical and rational person they've met, yet, I struggle a lot. I let myself cry and process all my emotions. Then I realize that I still am 24 years old and not 37, like in my dreams and I have my whole life ahead of me. I remember after all the haze has gone from my head, that I have completed my Master's in Architecture and last fall, I had started interning with a reputed firm in the East Village. I still have time to have a family, a career, and a partner I dreamt of. Life has given me a second chance and I need to seize the moment! Instead of mourning about a family that only existed in my head, I need to wake up and live the real life that is offered to me for a second time.

My mother and sister enter the room and we chat for a while making plans for the next week after I'll be discharged. I look at the painting in the hallway- bright yellow daisies just starting to bloom- and I smile to myself. They are a symbol of new beginnings and rebirth. Just like those daffodils, my life has just started blooming!

27

#Adventuregoneawry

by Vishakha Naware

Copy:
@rainbowsalt
posted 2h ago
"Living my best life"
<3 10,347

***

"What! Two hours and only 10,347 likes!" Sanya blubbered looking at her mobile phone with one of those expressions that resemble the 'disgust' emoji. She was used to getting at least a thousand more likes than that. This new and happening adventure that she had posted about was not that interesting! "People are getting bored with my updates. My life is over! I won't be an Insta star anymore. What would that be like? No more endorsements, no more free apparel, or free restaurant visits. I'd like to have to PAY for everything, ugh!" She grunted while rolling her eyes.

"And the worst part is that I'm stuck with 99k followers since last week. I was expecting it to reach 100k like yesterday," She screamed looking at her latest Apple iPhone

12 Pro Max which had a gold cover with a funny-looking unicorn on it and it had the words #rainbowsalt on it, duh!

"You need to like looking for a new adventure and stuff. Like really get out there. Give your followers the adventure they want!" Thea, her best friend, squeaked with her American-accent English. It was not her real accent, but both Sanya and she used it when they made Insta-videos attract more fans. "What kind of adventure, dude! I have done all the stuff possible: skydiving, bungee jumping, parasailing. You name it and I've done it. I even, like, lived without the internet for two whole hours, dude! That was some bitch-thing that anyone could have done," She rolled her eyes.

"Yeah, but that's like the 20th century! You need to get your thoughts on. Why don't you try something bizarre such as staying in a so-called haunted house or spending a night alone in the woods? That could be dope," Thea spoke without taking her eyes off her phone.

"Geez, Thea! I think you're onto something. One night in the woods... Alone... Now, that's something. I could do a photo-shoot – a pre-shoot, a post-shoot, and all that jazz!" Sanya said, jumping off her couch.

"Don't forget the "during" shoot, babe," Thea added.

"Duh!"- Sanya.

@rainbowsalt

Posted 1h ago

***

You guys! The day has arrived... Just an hour and I'm leaving for the woods! #gottagetspooky

<3 13,697

***

"Whoa! Whoa! Whoa! Just posted this and already 13k+ likes. This thing is working!" Sanya said, doing her little happy dance.

"I'm freaking out on the inside. What if some wild animal finds me and likes me enough as a snack? Dude, everyone knows I'm tasty! Oh God, I'm cracking lame jokes, that means I've crossed my level of craziness. But my followers don't need to know that. Wink. Wink," Sanya talked to herself in her Insta-emoji language.

She felt that she expressed herself better in emojis than in actual words. So, when she spoke, she spoke like: "OMG, that's horrible news. Sad face emoji."

Or "OMG that's awesome news, dancing emoji." That was her actual language- online and offline.

@rainbowsalt

Posted 30m ago

***

Ok, guys! Let's do this. Already roasting marshmallows on the campfire!

#joinmeinmyadventure

<3 12,984

***

"Life is saved. Just 30 minutes and 12k+ likes! I'm happy!" Sanya broke out into her happy dance again.

"Wait, what was that? That was spooky! Thea told me no animals live in this part of the woods. Well, at least her Google search did. Then why is this rustling noise coming?" Sanya said with beads of sweat trickling down her forehead. She looked here and there, but she saw no one or nothing! She felt that perhaps it was just her imagination. Being in nature was not her jam, but as promised to her fans, she had to try out something lit. And this was as lit as it could get. She ran inside her tent and shut the zip and held her head in her hands. She was trembling with fear, seeing shadows of things.

"It's just some small animal. Perhaps. Maybe a squirrel jumping around? Are squirrels nocturnal?" She was lost in her train of thoughts.

Thud!

@rainbowsalt

Posted 30m ago

***

You guys, the network here is sketchy and I just heard a loud thud. Hanging on to my life, hiding. Pray for me!!! #adventureinthewoods

She saw a shadow coming towards her tent. Did it look like an animal? No, no, it was a human being. A woman? No, no, it was a man. Who would wander here, in this part of the woods, at this hour? Sanya was super scared now. She felt like she should say something, but words didn't seem to leave her mouth.

She gathered enough courage and blurted out, "Who... Who is it?" Suddenly, the shadow was just outside the tent and in a moment, the zip started opening, and a man's head popped inside the tent. Sanya screamed for life!

"Shhh… Don't worry. It's fine. I am not going to hurt you. Just tell me, who are you and what are you doing here, that too alone, at this hour of the night?" The man, who was in his late thirties, said sharply. "Umm... It's my social media adventure project. I've decided to stay in the woods alone for a night," Sanya said without looking at him directly, her hands trembling with fear.

"What? Social media what? Anyway, it's good that I found you on time. Do you know how many drug-peddlers use this area for their crimes? I was on a lead and bumped into you. If anyone else would've spotted you before me, do you know what kind of consequences it may have had?" His voice was firm and concerned. Gathering courage Sanya looked at him and saw his police badge.

Now her mind was somewhat at rest. "Sorry, officer. It's just that I was losing my followers and had to do something extreme. You know how it is, being an Insta-star. There always has to be something new," She said somberly.

"No, I do not understand that. Anyway, it should not be at the cost of your life, should it now?" He asked.

"Of course not!" She nodded.

"Let's get you out of here to the nearby forest office," he said while opening the door to his jeep.

Sanya was dropped off by her friends and did not have her vehicle. "Thank you, officer," she said with teary eyes as she packed her stuff and folded her tent.

He dropped her near the forest office and said, "Listen, as I told you I'm following a lead, so I have to go now. You go inside the office and meet Mr. Janardhan, he will help you out and find someone to send you home. Okay?" "Yeah," she mumbled. "Excuse me, sir, can I quickly take a photo with you?"

"Oh, why not! Wow, what phone is this? Never seen anything like that?" He said curiously. Sanya answered him, took the photo, and thought of a new story she would tell her followers. Nobody needed to know what a scaredy-cat she had been. So she quickly uploaded the photo without even bothering about the filters.

@rainbowsalt

Posted moments ago.

***

The thud was from an animal and I had to run for my life. But this officer saved my life! New superhero

#superhero

New comment: Dude, but where's the officer?

***

"Hello, are you Mr. Janardhan?" Sanya spoke hesitatingly.

"Yes, but who are you? How did you reach here at this time?" He demanded. "Well, Mr. Prakash Sharma dropped me here. I was spending the night alone a few kilometres from here, near the big oak tree everyone talks about, and he somehow found me and told me it's unsafe due to the drug peddlers, so he dropped me here and told me that you'd arrange for me to return home," she explained. "What did you say? Prakash Sharma? Are you sure?" He was flabbergasted.

"Yeah, that's what his name was. Wait, I took a photo with him. Here!" She gave him her phone.

"I can only see you in this picture," he looked at her with worry.

"Wait, what? I swear I saw him next to me in the photo some time back. And now he's just gone! Something is wrong with my iPhone, I guess," she looked at her phone irritated.

"Miss, nothing is wrong with your phone. Prakash Sharma is dead for five years. He was shot near the spot you said you were camped at. He was chasing a lead to catch the drug-peddlers but was shot... While saving a woman who was held hostage by the gang. Luckily, he had called for back-up, so we could save the woman. Unfortunately, he died in the hospital a few days later," Janardhan explained, visibly shocked.

He described Prakash as a person who was tall, wheatish-skinned with a lean but strong body. He died when he was 37. Prakash was a bright police officer, who was also very kind. He was known for his benevolence and the way he treated everyone equally. All those details- his appearance and his character, matched with the person who Sanya had encountered in the woods. She was sweating profusely and her heart jumped in her body. She was petrified.

"Oh my God! So, I just met a…" Sanya said, so terrified, that she couldn't even complete the sentence.

"I don't know whether to believe you or not. Coz you Insta-stars are capable of imagining anything. But yes, I have to admit that it was kind of weird. Now let's get you home. Chetan, take out the office jeep and please drop this girl home," he shouted orders to Chetan, who was sitting in the other room and was oblivious to the whole thing.

@rainbowsalt

posted moments ago.

***

You guys! Taking a break from social media as I need to detox!!! Keep missing me.

#detoxfromsocialmedia

New comment: Adventure gone awry?

***

"You again?" Sanya looked at him exasperated. "Yes, I was just taking a stroll here. The air is so pure na?" he smiled at her. "But… They told me that you are d…d…dead," she stammered and looked at him slowly.

"Hahaha! Do I look dead to you?" he was amused.

"What's your name?" He asked her. "Sanya Mehta," she replied.

"Are you Anaya Mehta's daughter?" He questioned her.

"Yes, how do you know?" She was visibly surprised at that fact.

"No reason. See you around, I need to go now," he said walking away from her.

Suddenly Sanya felt numb. She remembered how her mom had disappeared for a couple of days and her dad and grandparents had looked for her everywhere. Sanya was 11 years old then. She didn't remember much as her dad had sent her to stay with her aunt in another city. She remembered when she returned home, the whole house was tense, yet relieved and her mother looked like she had undergone some trauma, but now she was happy to be back with her family. Sanya now remembered everyone's expressions after that incident. She was too young to understand what was going on. But now she understood. She suddenly felt at peace. The undead didn't scare her anymore now. She might even bump into them again while taking a stroll maybe.

28

An Alternate World

by Kristin Carmen

You would think that you know someone after being lifelong friends. Through sharing the ups and downs of life, but that isn't always the case. Sometimes, you realize that you barely knew them, and sometimes they barely even knew themselves.

It was a lifetime of knowing each other. Anisa and Ajay had known each other since they were 6 years old. Both grew up near each other and attended the same schools and classes as well as their fathers being great friends. Now, decades later, they were still close and had families of their own to raise.

After a few years apart, they began to hang out together again. Both families joined on vacations and all sorts of social outings. It was a beautiful reunion, especially with the kids being so close in age. A deep bond between the two families formed. Until, one day, things started to change.

Anisa could tell things weren't quite right between Ajay and his wife Bela. Although neither would they ever say there were any issues, Anisa could tell that her friends were tense.

Still, everything went on the same as usual. Until one day Ajay came over to vent.

Ajay began to explain, "Bela and I have been having a few problems and she wants a divorce." Tears started streaming out of his eyes.

Anisa could see that he was bewildered as to why. He seemed depressed and confused about what to do regarding his situation. She tried to console her friend as best as she could. He agreed that things would eventually work out and then excused himself to the bathroom. On his way, he reached into a bag that he brought with him.

As he reached into the bag he stated, "I forgot to take my heart medication."

Grabbing two pill bottles, he quickly made his way out of the room. Anisa thought nothing of it.

A few minutes lapsed and Ajay came back and sat down and continued. "I took a bunch of pills."

Odd, Anisa thought. But where were his other pills? He sat quietly for a while before speaking. Anisa thought that he was only trying to think things through.

Then Ajay made a strange comment, "I just swallowed hundreds of pills." He sounded strange.

Anisa was confused. Then Ajay started to get up and slumped over. Anisa ran to the bottles he put back in his bag. Two empty bottles. They were full when he excused himself.

And neither were heart medications. They were strong narcotics. Oh no! Anisa thought to herself. He's trying to commit suicide! She was in shock but knew to call the paramedics right away.

After a short description of what transpired, the medics were there in two minutes. Thankfully the hospital was relatively close. Although those two minutes felt like an eternity, she was relieved that they came so soon.

The medics took him and Anisa gathered her belongings and met them at the hospital. Her friend almost died on the way but they were able to resuscitate him. She was told that those pills induced a coma and those pills probably would not push him over his deathbed.

Anisa spent the next week going back and forth to the hospital as her friend laid there in a coma. Doctors still were not sure if he would live, even if so, how much of his brain would recover. Those pills were not strong enough to push him to death but were lethal enough to have terrible side effects. It was a very stressful week.

Eventually, her friend did come through and after many tests, the doctors believed that Ajay would make a full recovery.

Ajay was finally released from the hospital, and Anisa took him to her home. There she thought he could recover better with the help from her and her family. Anisa's husband wasn't thrilled about the idea, but he understood and Ajay had become a close friend of his as well.

Unfortunately, neither Anisa nor her husband realized the extent of their friend's issues. It soon became apparent that things were not quite well. Ajay's moods and personality would change a lot. It was as if he was going in and out of doors in his mind. She couldn't tell who she was talking to from one minute to the next.

For hours they would sit and talk. Ajay would be his normal self and then switch gears saying that he wanted to kill everyone, then he would say he felt guilty and ashamed of his childhood.

Then back to normal, then completely quiet, and then Ajay would say, "They want me to kill myself."

Anisa kept wondering who 'They' were.

After a lot of encouragement, Ajay finally sought psychological support. At first, he did not say much about it. He made it sound like it was just depression. But soon, the truth came out.

One day, while Anisa's husband was at work and the kids were at school. Ajay started having another confusing episode. He told Anisa that he was in love with her, that it was all her fault.

Anisa had no clue what he was talking about. He went on and on about how he was always in love with her since they were young children. Then Ajay abruptly switched gears and started explaining the horrible abuse he endured as a child. It was a lot for Anisa to wrap her head around, but she did her best to stay calm. Cool heads prevail, she reminded herself.

She tactfully talked to Ajay about his feelings and the disclosures he was making. She always thought he had been abused as a child but never knew how intense it was. Everything was starting to make more sense now. Anisa asked why it seemed as if he was walking through doors and changing personalities. Did he know why?

It turns out, he did. Ajay explained that his psychologist said he had multiple personality disorder (MPD). He further explained that 'he' the alter personalities were homicidal and the host personality was homicidal too.

Ajay was a matter of fact in relaying his diagnosis. It was like he had no feelings about it.

Blankly he said, "I didn't even realize that I had MPD all these years." And immediately after what he said, he started speaking frantically. "They're now yelling at me that I have to kill you."

Then he went on further saying that they were also telling him to kill other people and rambled off names of people that they both knew.

Anisa was scared. It sounded like he meant it. Ajay had everything mapped out how he was going to kill everyone and then kill himself. She did not understand what was happening to him. Ajay must have seen the look of fear in her eyes. He immediately ran out of the house.

She was relieved he left, but at the same time, she was scared to death for herself, him, and the others. She called the crisis hotline but was told there was nothing anyone could do unless he attempted to her, himself, or others. Anisa couldn't believe that there was nothing anyone could or would do to further help him.

Later, she received a call from a mutual friend of hers, Brian. He told Anisa and her husband that Ajay had threatened his life with a knife and a fight ensued. Her friend was extremely angry and upset as he had just opened up his home to have Ajay stay with him. Ajay lied and said Anisa threw him out. Brian also said Ajay had been telling him and all their friends that Anisa and Ajay were secretly engaged for months as well as many other lies, he had been telling others for years about her.

Anisa was now really upset. She didn't realize her friend was doing that behind her back all those years. Now, not only did she have a friend with psychosis that wanted to kill her, himself, and others, but now all these lies to contend with.

Anisa called some of her other mutual friends. Sure enough, Ajay was saying all those things to all their mutual friends. One by one, Anisa called and explained the truth. Unfortunately, her friends were not as understanding about Ajay's illness and were furious about the lies…

The next day, she received a call from Ajay's wife, Bela. She explained that Ajay tried to commit suicide again. This time he did not blame it on Bela like before. This time he was telling everyone it was because Anisa broke off their engagement.

Anisa was mortified and tried to explain everything to Bela. Bela stopped her in the middle of the explanation. "I know, I know, dear. The reason I left him was that I found out and knew that he was lying about everything. I didn't want to upset you, so I didn't say anything."

Bela let out a deep sigh, "It's been going on for a while now, and I was afraid for me and the children. I didn't realize that it was this serious. I'm so sorry."

Bela knew! But then again, Anisa realized that she knew and didn't tell anyone as well. There are so many stigmas towards mental illness that she didn't want people to treat her friend badly. She was trying to be respectful of his privacy. They all were.

And here many people's lives were In jeopardy as well as his. Ajay was released by the hospital immediately. No psychological restrictions nor assistance despite the dangers to himself and others.

During the week that followed, Anisa heard through others that Ajay was telling everyone that Anisa was at fault for the second suicide attempt. Luckily, no one believed him this time. Anisa never heard from Ajay ever again after that.

Maybe someone's life can always end up being bigger than a normal question mark we put at the end of our queries out of curiosity. The curiosity that will always absorb every part within us and leave our bodies to decay with some rotting temperaments and delusional emotions that can never be at peace. The peace that one's soul always craved for since the person's life started hanging on the strings that can be pulled by an unknown character piled up with God knows how more in that pack, to spur the sentiments drowning around a place like a black hole.

29

Unforgiven

by Kristin Carmen

How to forget the unforgettable? They say that revenge is sweeter than surrender. A truce can never be won. Those who were born mad have a taste for it. But then again, the story has just begun.

Two long years she waited. Two very long years. Veronica thought back. Her mind was racing. Only if she could alleviate the pain in her head it caused.

Veronica Zalik started coming to my office about a month ago. Originally, she was just complaining of migraines and bouts of rage that she had been experiencing after being kidnapped in a dungeon of sorts a couple of years back. Since our initial meeting, it had come to my attention that there was more there beneath what she showed on the surface.

Veronica was also displaying signs of anti-social behaviour and the effects of psychological torture, which is not uncommon for someone who had gone through trauma as she endured. For the most part, she seemed like a normal, happy 30-year-old woman.

She had briefly touched on a couple of traumatic events in her childhood. Rich, abusive parents who demanded perfection. An accident as a toddler that she did not quite remember that had caused brain trauma during a car accident. And being taunted by the kids at school for having some type of kinetic sixth sense. She refused to describe what exactly that entailed, however.

Nothing seemed unusual, she dressed and kept herself tidy. She was very sure of herself and intelligent as well.

She decided during the last session that she was going to talk about what happened in the dungeon. I could see she seemed to have a lot on her mind. So I asked if she was ready to talk about it during the session.

"Veronica, do you still want to talk about what happened in the dungeon?"

She looked distracted.

"Veronica?"

"Oh, yeah. Yes," she replied. Veronica rubbed her head. She was eager to get this out of her head and into the open.

"They just grabbed me and shoved me in a van."

"Who grabbed you? Where were you at that time?" I asked.

"Well, I don't know. These strange men. I got off the plane and was waiting for my brother to pick me up from the airport."

"Okay… And then what happened?"

I couldn't tell what her emotions were, it just seemed flat. So I let her continue.

"Umm… I was on my way back from Heathrow and arrived at the Orlando International Airport on time. My brother, Sean, said he would pick me up, but he never called and he never showed up. I waited over an hour. I called and called, but he never answered any of my calls. I was exhausted from the flight, so I decided to call a cab. The cab driver said he couldn't pick me up at the airport and I was instructed to take the shuttle to a business area where he could pick me up. The area I waited at had a bunch of warehouses and a couple of small businesses, but they were mainly vacant. I thought it would be a busy public area, but it was just the opposite."

Then Veronica continued, again without any emotion, "A car pulled up. The driver said I would have to share the cab with another fare. I was nervous to get out of the area, so I said okay. I got into the back seat, the man sitting next to me politely smiled and turned to look out the window. The driver started driving, and I felt comfortable. The driver stopped at the next light, still all vacant businesses and warehouses. Then the man next to me pulled out a gun, shoved it into my ribs, and told me not to say anything. So I didn't. The driver got out and opened my door and blindfolded me. It didn't seem like we were in the car that long and then they pushed me into a room and tied me to a post."

"Oh!" I said, worried about how she was doing emotionally. "Do you want to explain more?"

Veronica without blinking continued. "Yes. Not much happened for a long time. Days I think. They just shoved food in and didn't say anything." Veronica looked confused and rubbed her head some more. Staring blankly, she continued. "Eventually, one came in and just started to call me names and sliced a knife into my skin. He said I was his property now. He didn't do anything else, just left afterward."

I thought to myself, how odd that was. I looked at Veronica. She was wearing a short-sleeve shirt and skirt. Not a mark on her. "These men didn't want anything from you or try to have sex with you?"

Veronica replied, "No."

She rubbed her head some more. "I figured I was being held for ransom or something like that."

"And how long did this continue?" I was curious now.

"Two years." She said.

Wow. "Two years and nothing else happened during that time besides cutting you, calling you names, and feeding you? Did you try to escape during that time?"

"That's all. Nothing else."

Veronica's emotions and eyes were still apathetic. I tried to escape when I heard one telling the other one that they were going to kill me. I thought my brother would have saved me by then. I don't understand why he didn't pay the ransom."

"Was there a ransom, Veronica? How much?"

Veronica started looking agitated and her answer was sharp and forceful. "I don't know. I thought..."

I figured I would calm her down by asking how she got away. Veronica explained that she willed the ropes to untie, somehow they just untied and she ran. She eventually found someone who had a phone and called her brother to get her.

"Did he ever come and got you?"

There was no light in her eyes, and Veronica gave a quiet but sharp, "Yes."

"Did you ever get a chance to ask him about the ransom?"

Veronica gave out a loud huff and slammed her hand on the desk, "NO!" She yelled angrily. Then she started walking out the door.

"Wait!" I called her out. Veronica turned around, rubbed her head, and looked calm again like nothing happened.

"Should I ask someone to get something for you?"

"I was just wondering if you ever found out where the dungeon was located."

"Yeah, it was on 42nd Upper East Street. A few blocks from the airport."

"Oh, okay. I will note it down. Is it possible for you to bring your brother with you in the next session?"

Veronica looked confused. "No, he won't be able to make it. He's tied up right now and I don't think he will be around much longer."

"Oh? May I ask why?"

Veronica smiled and didn't respond. She walked out and shut the door behind her.

Something about her triggered me and now I am drowning in anxiousness and I knew that there must be more to the story. It didn't make sense to me. Her behaviour was erratic in a different way than I would expect from a trauma standpoint.

So, I decided to drive to the address where Veronica said the incident happened during my lunch break. Oddly, it was only a block from the police station. So I went in to inquire as to whether or not reports were filed.

No report. I asked the police officer if it would be okay to look around the abandoned warehouse at the address she gave me. The police escorted me to the site.

We all could hear a strange muffled sound coming from one of the rooms. We went in and found a man tied to a post. A rag shoved in his mouth and he had slice marks carved all over him. The police took the ragout and cut the ropes off of him.

They asked who did this to him. He said his sister was going to kill him. Her name was Veronica Zalik. I couldn't tell if I was surprised or not.

I listened as the police questioned the gentleman some more. He said that his sister had been having problems for about two years with symptoms of migraines, fits of rage, anti-social behaviours, and delusional thoughts of persecution. It started after her boyfriend left her because Veronica was psychologically and physically abusing him. Veronica turned it around to be her brother's fault and thought everyone was out to get her. She never accepted responsibility for her actions.

According to her brother, Veronica tied him up because he once told her boyfriend to break up with her. She was now planning to get revenge by killing him and her ex-boyfriend. Her brother, Sean, further explained that since Veronica was a kid, she thought she was one of the characters in a Marvel Comic book. She had always had a fascination with the X-Men. He said they were always at odds because he loved DC Comics. They always played superheroes growing up. Sean was Mister Zsasz and Veronica was Phoenix.

Except, Sean said, "She got lost in that world somehow and always thought I would save her. But I was the villain, and I couldn't."

The police then took the rest of the report from Sean, and I was told to go home and the police department would be in contact with me.

Today, I came down to the police station to file my statement. The police explained to me that Veronica Zalik had already murdered her boyfriend earlier on the day we found Sean tied up. The boyfriend was found with the initials "VZ" carved into him and the police believed she carved her initials on his wrist, so he would never forget anything about her or leave her again. I was told that in her file it states that she believes her ex-boyfriend is still alive and lives with her. She never could accept the fact that he left her.

It also stated that she had made a report years ago with the police department under an alias name, Jean Elaine Grey, the fictional name of Phoenix, and she was kidnapped after getting off a plane 10 years ago. She had been abused physically and psychologically by the assailants. One even carved his initials on her backside. When I looked at the police photo, I saw the initials "VZ" carved into her backside. They never found the men. It was the same VZ that was carved in her boyfriend. But why would she?

I finished my statement and left. I walked to the corner cafe to grab a coffee in hopes of abating my headache. I grabbed my cup and took a seat at the table looking towards the abandoned warehouse across the street.

Oddly enough, as I am sitting down, I see a copy of an old Batman comic book "The Shadow of The Bat" lying on the table.

Wow, there is the name Mister Zsasz. That is the character Sean was talking about. It is an interesting storyline, the fictional name of Mister Zsasz is Victor Zsasz.

"VZ?"

Wait, what!?

30

The Unveiling

by Kristin Carmen

It wasn't always this way, she thought to herself, or was it? Liza couldn't tell if life has always been this way or if the frailties of existence were somehow catching up with her these days.

Theirs was a beautiful friendship that had turned into an amazing romance, she was so happy that they were going to get married. Liza had looked forward to living the rest of her life with Wilson. She could finally put all the nightmares of her past behind and start a new life and have a family of her own. It was her time. It was her one true dream.

But that was then. If only we could skip to the later chapters of our lives. If only we could see ahead to the triumphs and pitfalls that await us. The harsh reality is that we cannot. We make the best decisions we can with the information and experiences known at the time. We live each day in hopes of a better tomorrow.

Every day she ends up where she wishes that she could go back, go back to change all those little decisions she had made a long time ago. Liza wished that she could have trusted her instincts more than her heart and trusted herself more than others. Sometimes there are no red flags. Sometimes all you have is this little voice inside your gut saying that something is not quite right. She wished that she understood this back then.

Liza did not listen to that little voice and she ended up paying the price. Now every time she looked at her daughter, Caroline, she was reminded of what that choice had cost her.

Everything started perfectly in her marriage until the day Liza found out that she was pregnant and was having her first child. It all felt like a beautiful dream.

Up until then, she and Wilson worked, played like kids, and enjoyed their own company as well as their friends and family. They were well-known members of their community. Life couldn't have been better.

Then one day, it was as if someone had snapped their fingers; life changed in an instant.

Wilson came home from work, as usual, grabbed his beer out of the refrigerator, and started telling Liza about his day at work. He was happy and jovial as usual. After he had finished telling her of the day's events, she decided to tell him the amazing news.

Liza was so excited to tell Wilson. She could hardly believe it herself. For years, the doctors had been telling her that she could never have children. She and Wilson had planned to adopt a kid shortly. So she couldn't wait to tell her husband.

"I found out something amazing today." She turned to look at him in the eyes, glowing from the happiness that ran through her.

"Oh?" He played along.

"What is the thing you found that made you so chirpy?" Wilson was curious to know what his wife was up to now.

A huge grin appeared on Liza's face as she said, "Well I found out that we are going to have a baby!"

Wilson almost choked on his beer and looked at her in massive surprise. "Wait, what! You can't have children though, how? What?"

Liza couldn't tell if he was happy, angry, or just in complete shock at that moment. Something didn't feel right. She began to explain that the doctor said her scarring healed enough so that she could now have kids. She was indeed pregnant with their first child.

Wilson just went completely quiet and stared for the rest of the evening at the TV set. He didn't eat nor moved until he went to bed. For some reason, even when he crawled into bed with her that night, it felt cold to Liza. Wilson did not touch her or talk to her. He just went to sleep.

The following day, Wilson left for work as usual. Liza had decided to cook his favorite meal in hopes to smooth things over between them. But when he came home later that evening, he didn't say a word to Liza. He just grabbed the chili bowl and headed for his chair in front of the TV. He sat down and started eating. Liza was silent not knowing what to think. The air felt still for some reason.

Halfway through eating, Wilson throws the chili at her. Breaking the bowl on the countertop behind her. A near miss. Liza was in shock and froze in her tracks, afraid of moving. He started screaming that the chili was horrible and saying a bunch of derogatory remarks about her cooking.

Then Wilson came towards her screaming in her face. She apologized for the food. Then he pushed her. She became frightened for the baby and ran for the front door. He grabbed her and blocked the door. Then he started banging as hard as he could into her stomach each time. She just tried her level best to beat him up and fight back.

She ferociously asked him to just get out of the house. And get back when he will stabilize his volatile mindset. Wilson never came back.

Then soon enough she found out that she was having twins, but one of the twins died from the abuse. The other twin was still alive but the placenta was broken. She spent the rest of the pregnancy hoping her child would survive. Liza lost a lot of blood and her heart nearly gave out during delivery, but it was all worth it when she looked into the eyes of her beautiful baby girl.

"Throughout the pregnancy, until my little angel, Caroline was born, I had some hope that maybe Wilson will come back and accept us. Accept me and our newborn with the beautiful smile that was brighter than the sun and as soothing as the moon." She confessed to her sister Carol.

Liza still remembers how heartbroken he was when the doctor originally said that they couldn't have a baby. And growing Caroline up into this gorgeous young lady, was such a delight. She always thought maybe Wilson had a reason he left. Maybe he only wanted to take some time.

But now Caroline is 16 years old. Liza and Caroline live in the same house which is however just the same way as Wilson left it to be. That frame from their wedding is still intact on the fireplace mantel, moreover, each and everything is in place till now. With the hope that Wilson will somehow get back to them.

Liza always explained while showing Caroline the frames of how hard-working and amazing her father is. She never uttered a word about a minor flaw in Wilson. All Liza had to talk about was Wilson and Carol, her elder sister.

Caroline saw her mom crying out loud, and once again Liza explained everything about Wilson. Caroline never heard in detail about her father's name but this time it was the hardest mental breakdown a 16-year-old little kid could ever tackle. Because whenever Wilson's name would come up, Liza was always pouring her eyes out.

Caroline knew how to tackle her mother, but this time it was harsh to see her this way, so she had to call her aunt. Her aunt was out for some little chores and Caroline was glad that she was only two blocks away and it wasn't difficult for her to reach out as soon as she could.

Seriously after 15 years, Caroline came to know that Liza was still hung up on Wilson.

Caroline with tears in her eyes summarized each and everything, "Aunt Carol can you call up my dad. Because it's not the first-time mom is crying this way. She told me not to tell you about my dad, Wilson. Or show you those frames of her marriage. I'm always questionable about those frames. But I never dared to ask anyone about it. I know we live together with you but she hid everything so well."

Carol was still absorbing the fact that Caroline took out the frames again which were empty. She surmised that her sister was getting worse and may need to go back to the hospital again. Carol let out a long deep sigh.

Carol explained each and everything to Caroline with a heavy heart, "Liza was never married, no one around her knew Wilson. She had you from another man named,

Christopher, they were not even married. Moreover, Liza just lived with Christopher for 6 months. Whatever happened between them and how it all started was just a mishap and he just left her the moment he came to know about the baby. But she always pictured him as Wilson, her husband. The same Wilson who never existed, the same Wilson who had no reason to prevail in Liza's life. When she was about to have twins, then Christopher left her alone, because he tried his level best to make her understand that he is not Wilson. But now he had enough of her picturing him as her husband moreover, there was never a Wilson in the first place."

Carol continued, "We both told you about the other twin, right? The other twin in her body growing up was unable to survive because of some complications during her pregnancy. And not because of Wilson. I never knew why that empty frame is in the house or why Christopher was Wilson to her. The same Christopher who wasn't around her throughout her pregnancy, the same Christopher she thought was her husband Wilson."

Caroline was in shock. All she ever knew of her father is now completely changed. It felt like she had a bad dream.

Caroline summoned up the courage and asked Carol, "Is it possible to find or contact Christopher?"

Carol explained that she had heard Christopher had passed away while at war when Caroline was 12 years old.

"I will dig up the obituary I found and bring it to you. I think that your mother already knew about his death. Caroline, your mom has been having problems like this since she was 25 years old. I guess it is time to bring her back to the hospital."

Caroline remembers going to the hospital with her grandmother a few years back. Her grandmother never talked about it, however. Caroline was so happy to have her mother back that she never asked what happened.

Out of suspicion, she inquired, "Why mom said that you know that she talks to Wilson quite often. I have heard her talk to him too. I never wanted to talk to him."

Carol looked at her and said nothing. Carol's silence cleared the blurry fact. At last, Carol took her to the doctor and explained all the details of what she was going on for the last 16 years. She told the doctor that Liza was mentally stable and functioning well, but a corner of her mind was picturing an imaginary identity named Wilson with whom she talked to as her daughter informed. Carol further explained that Liza was prescribed medication from that particular doctor who strictly asked Liza to follow those medications, 15 years ago. She took it for a year until she lived with me. I never knew she stopped those pills and is back to that phase."

Caroline was numb. She had no words anymore. No words to spill out, she just felt a chilling sensation down her spine. Is that why she never said anything to anyone about her mother? Or was it because she too saw a man and wife in what everyone else said was an empty frame. Caroline always thought that it was Wilson who she heard talking to her in her mind. Now she was confused.

Who would ever know why Caroline never questioned her mom about those empty frames. The empty frames that had no identity. Did she hear and believe her mom talking to a person aka her so-called dad?

ACKNOWLEDGMENTS

I will always be thankful to my parents and my sister and the people with whom I grew up with. Seeing that glimmer in their eyes is all that cheers me up. I can start naming all of them who pushed me up a notch and do what I do. But it always starts from within right. I will always be indebted to all of you. And grateful for the memories of the corridors of my school where I crossed paths with an amazing person. Moreover, our book would be nothing if all of the co-authors never brought their amazing work here. Of course, I am so delighted by the warmth of the Inkfeathers team.

Meet the
Co-Authors

Tejasvee Nagar

Tejasvee is a 17-year-old high school student who has an instinct for writing. Writing followed her after she developed the art of passive reading, gazing around book pages like they are stars and through games like crosswords. On a sunny day, she might also swipe up and style dark academia outfits. She has a keen interest in Greek mythology that you could already find with her Instagram username. She paints a world through her quill. She is a music lover at heart too. You can follow her at @eurydicelived on Instagram, Twitter and Tumblr for long aesthetic poems and music related posts.

Deepika Ganu

Deepika Ganu is a Risk Management Professional from Mumbai. The story in this book is more like a walk through the main theme as how are the life's moments unfold the secrets and give us new belief. She loves connecting and finds her inspiration truly from penning down beautiful thoughts, capturing the best moments and memories across. She made her debut in story telling anthology "Locked in Tales" by Did You Read Today that opened up in lockdown. Deepika is an avid reader and a blogger. She blogs about her experiences, memories, beautiful quotes and is best known for her simple write-ups packed with deep insights.

Karen Pereira

Karen Pereira, a twenty-year-old student pursuing her degree in management studies, has been writing for the past five years and is currently working as a content writer. She has published her own anthology titled 'After Hours' that has ranked 24 in the Amazon bestsellers list. These 14 short horror stories revolve around her nightmares, bringing them to life through detailed story telling. She has written for notable presses like The Bandra Buzz, The Times of India and Youth Magazine to name a few. With an excellent grasp of the language, evident from competitions that she has won in school and on college level, she has breathed life into her stories, giving the readers a unique experience. She hopes to continue her dream of storytelling, thereby inspiring young authors everywhere.

Rosalind Reshma

Rosalind Reshma is an educator, storyteller, mother and over thinker who spends her day teaching the nuances of language to young, brilliant minds. When she is not doing that she writes poems and stories. She spent her childhood in Imphal and  she believes that the beautiful landscape and the interaction of wonderful people there played a great role in developing her imagination and love for literature. She holds a bachelor's degree in English Literature, a master's in Applied Linguistics and has an M.Phil in Translation studies. She has authored a chapbook, Lost Interpretations (2017) and a collection of short stories, Phantom Listeners (2020). She lives in Hyderabad with her family- two humans and her gorgeous cats.

Anamika Kundu

Anamika Kundu is the daughter of an Army Officer, who married another and proudly calls herself an Indian, belonging to the nation. Having been a teacher who has taught not only English but a handful of other subjects, for nearly a quarter of a century she feels teaching is her calling. She loves stories, to read, write or teach. An ardent outdoor lover, she has dabbled in sports and games from equestrian to badminton to yoga and of late has taken to running half marathons. She resides in Pune with her husband. During the Pandemic she discovered her passion for writing and is grateful to #Didyoureadtoday and #Didyouwritetoday to help her hone her skills. Her work can be seen at lifestrialsandsuccesses.com

Prajitha Ravipati

Prajitha Ravi is an Earthian, smile is her accessory and tries everyone around her to wear it. An infant in writing. And taking it step by step and the writing journey of her started with "Little Things" published in an Anthology "Twilight" by Mohnish Karanam.

"Keep Going" mantra is what she believes in.

Vaibhav Koktare

Vaibhav Koktare is a budding author from Thane, Maharashtra. He is currently pursuing his Master's in History from University of Mumbai. His passion for writing began in school days and as of today he has authored numerous stories on 'Pratilipi Marathi' app garnering more than 100K reads from his devoted readers. His writing explores genres of horror, mystery and thriller. Up till now he has written in Marathi language and 'Reflection' marks his first step towards the English language. Explore more of his writings on 'Pratilipi Marathi' app. Some of his stories also available in audio format on YouTube and 'Pratilipi FM' app. You can connect with him on Instagram @__vaibhav_vk__ and his page @__goodh_kalamkar__

Kanchan Hiranandani

Kanchan Hiranandani is a poet, writer, and a Delhi based entrepreneur. She is BSc chemistry honours and holds an MBA degree in HR from Banasthali Vidhyapith, Jaipur. She worked as a banker. She is passionate about nature and writing. She is a part of many anthologies like success ladder, The Tale Of Enigmas, Lost and Misunderstood, Frightening Stories, Magical Mellow, India Needs Change, etc.

Rutika Pandya

A 24-year-old girl from Ahmedabad, India, Rutika is pursuing MSc. Forensic Science. As a voracious reader, she learnt that words could provide a comfortable place to a soul searching for peace and belonging within this chaotic word. She has been constantly trying to juggle between reading and writing. You'll mostly find her recommending "The Book Thief" to every reader out there. Take this as a sign and go fall in love with Zusak's words.

Swikriti Lahoty

Swikriti is a sports physiotherapist who has always been into words, literature, another world which is full of fiction, and people she wishes actually existed in the real world. She treats patients in the day and weaves words in the night. She founded a page The Literature Studio with a couple of friends to promote and give a platform to other writers, the one she would have liked early on to encourage her to write more. Her career and writing are her passion, her life and she wishes to explore every aspect of it. This is her first short story and hopefully, not the last. Happy reading!

Dipali Talwar

She is a CA student who finds solace in the stories and tales of life. She likes to think about the wonders of the little moments. This is her second anthology where she tries to let the reader feel the untold and unfelt. We often tend to ignore our dilemmas but the toll they take on us is huge. In this story, Dipali takes you through one of Vrinda's experiences.

Muskan Kamwani

Muskan Kamwani is an eloquent writer. She believes in the magic of ink. She embraces light, dark, and the beauty of pain. She is on a way to see a world full of curious and compassionate people. Writing is the only thing that keeps her sane and makes her feel most alive.

Shaymi Shah

Shaymi Shah is a freelance architect by profession and a creative content writer by passion. Most of her writing comes from the observations of everyday life. She tends to have an inclination towards seeing the otherwise common things that happen in life with a different perspective. Today, through a lot of practice, she has successfully imbibed in herself the skill of weaving stories-

stories that one can easily lose themselves in. She has written for 15 anthologies so far and is taking a step at a time to make her dream of having her solo book published come to reality.

Manoj Vaz

Manoj Vaz is an award-winning copywriter with 3 decades of experience handling over 50 blue-chip clients. Post a premature retirement, he has published six books; Tinsel - a hard look at Mumbai's Show Biz, The Kidnapping and The Meth Mystery - both for teenagers, Kaleidoscope - short stories and poems, and Random Musings - original quotes. Queendom - his latest historical offering is garnering unprecedented interest and is set to be a bestseller.

Honey Patel

Honey is a dentist from Gujarat with sheer love for words and creating poetry. She thinks words heal people and can definitely make the world a better place to live in. Her goal is to spread kindness and smiles with her words.

Nitya Saini

Nitya Saini has now upgraded from "just a computer science majors" to a Content Writer, in 2021 only. This is her second time working with Inkfeathers. Her life is more or less similar to other people who have recently started working, except she is still a college student at heart and is known for lightening up the mood of people burdened by the weight of the most non-anticipated day, i.e. deadline.

Mansi Gupta

Educator by profession, writer by passion and an ardent food enthusiast, Mansi Gupta has over 18 years of experience in the field of education. Her recent story- 'Love in the times of a Pandemic' was published in the Anthology –'Locked in Tales'. She is currently working on multiple anthologies. Mansi has been teaching children of all age groups and special learning needs, her methodologies have been immensely successful in building academic competencies in kids with ADHD, dyslexia and partial deafness. Her differential learning techniques eminently helped bring joy and enthusiasm in the lives of many children and adolescents facing loss of learning appetite. Mansi holds a M.Sc. degree in Counselling and Psychotherapy and another in Clinical Research. A witty mother of two adorable sons, she aspires that her writing convinces her husband to move his career from editing to Movie Direction. Having received many accolades in different writing groups, Mansi shares her knowledge and expertise through her online Instagram page called @letsraisehappykids and her personal Instagram handle is @mansinipungupta.

Dewni De Silva

Born and brought up in the beautiful islands of Sri Lanka, Dewni is a mad-hatter when it comes to books and writing. Her first Anthology was published in "The Forgotten Sagas." When she isn't reading or writing, she loves to talk about contemporary issues and aesthetic designs.

Ranjna Gopal

Ranjna is a British born London author. Second outing with Inkfeathers Publishing. Mother of five and health professional I live a very busy life but always make time for my sanctuary which is home with a notepad and pen. No laptops for me.

Munmun Aidasani

Munmun Aidasani, Chartered Financial Analyst by profession, hails from city of lakes, Bhopal (India) currently residing in Dubai (U. A. E). She loves wearing many hats. She is an avid and a versatile writer, an author, and a blogger. A dreamer with passion to establish her own benchmark in writing. When she is not writing, she indulges her children, husband and loved-ones with sumptuous food, with a curious mind trying to witness art in everything possible and in quest of exploring new horizons.

Her inner wisdom of being empathic and caring towards her loved-ones makes her the best human being around. She loves writing fictional as well as reality-based inspiring articles. She wants to spread her wings in each genre and believes in versatility. She can be reached at

Instagram: @munmunaidasani

Facebook page: Rising-Mom

Email: aidasanimunmun@gmail.com

Sumeet Doondani

Sumeet Doondani is an amateur writer, a graduate in the field of pharmacy who's currently helping his dad in his profession along with self-made pharmacy setup. His hobbies include writing, reading, counselling, motivating, traveling, caring and sharing joys around. He says: 'Life is a misery, bizarre secrets lie in the darkest depths, so be wise and kind to all, love and gratitude for all.' He can be reached on Instagram @ursumeet.

Vaishali Chandorkar Chitale

An alumna of the Indian Institute of Mass Communication, New Delhi, Vaishali Chandorkar Chitale, is an English (Hons) graduate from Hindu College, Delhi University. She is a free-lance journalist, educationist, author and a poet. She likes to write about her life, anecdotes and fiction. She firmly believes in the saying, that 'if you want the rainbow, you have to put up with the rain' Her stories have been published in paperback anthologies, e-books, and on online portals of StoryMirror.com and Bonobology.com. She has also taught English in many schools and retired from Delhi Public school, Pune in 2004 after a career of over 14 years to pursue her passion for writing. You can follow her on her blog www.anenviablejourney.wordpress.com. She can be reached at vchandorkar@gmail.com.

Vishakha Naware

Vishakha Naware is your typical working mom, juggling work and family! Former journalist and a German language trainer by profession, her passion lies in languages, reading, and writing short stories! A self-proclaimed Master-Chef, she loves experimenting with new recipes. She loves to travel and explore new places and cultures. She's a full-time mom to a six-year-old active primary schooler. And when she's not running after him for finishing his homework, she likes to binge-watch dramas, thrillers and comedies on Netflix and likes to get lost in the world of books.

Kristin Carmen

Kristin Carmen is a Paralegal out of Florida, USA. She is an inspirational writer and poet. Kristin has spent the last decade reading and writing on a diverse genre of topics.

She has recently become a short story writer in several anthologies and publications.

INKFEATHERS PUBLISHING

India's Most Author Friendly Publishing House

Stay updated about latest books, anthologies, events, exclusive offers, contests, product giveaways and other things that we do to support authors.

 Inkfeathers Publishing

 @InkfeathersPublishing

 @_Inkfeathers

 @Inkfeathers

 Inkfeathers.com

We'd love to connect with you!